PHANTOM DRIFT

A JOURNAL OF NEW FABULISM

ISSUE 8: *Hidden Planets, Monster Stars*

Phantom Drift Limited   Issue Eight
Portland, Oregon   Fall, 2018

PHANTOM DRIFT
A Journal of New Fabulism

Editorial Board

ISSN: 2162-8211
ISBN: 978-0-9964426-3-3

Matt Schumacher, Managing Editor
Martha Bayless, Fiction Co-Editor
Miranda Schmidt, Fiction Co-Editor
Mary Lenoir Bond, Poetry Co-Editor / Social Media Editor
John Morrison, Poetry Co-Editor
Elizabeth Schumacher, Poetry Co-Editor
Peter Grandbois, Contributing Editor
David Memmott, Contributing Editor
Ki Russell, Contributing Editor
Leslie What, Contributing Editor

Design & Layout: *Kristin Summers, redbat design*

Issue Eight Cover Art: *"After Rain" by Naoto Hattori (www.naotohattori.com)*

Phantom Drift Limited is a 501(c)(3) tax-exempt organization founded to develop an understanding of and appreciation for fabulist literature. *Phantom Drift* is one of the few literary journals in the United States focused on fabulist writing. We aim to nurture the literature of fabulism, the fantastic, and the surreal by publishing an appealing, top-quality literary journal featuring only the best short stories, poetry, and critical thinking on fabulism by established, emerging, and new writers from the U.S. and abroad. Our support for writers takes the form of not only providing a showcase for their works, but offering payment, a practice that both assures us the best of writers' work and supports literature as a whole. The journal will be published annually in the fall (October). Donations are deductible to the extent allowed by law. Orders, subscriptions and donations can be made on-line at www.phantomdrift.org.

Direct mail orders can be made by sending check or money order for $15 (postage paid) to:

Phantom Drift
PO Box 31001
Portland, OR 97231

Phantom Drift accepts on-line submissions from January 1 – April 30.

PHANTOM CROSSING

THE FANTASTIC MEETS THE ANTHROPOCENE:
AN INTRODUCTION TO ISSUE EIGHT

A vast strangeness invades our precessions from deep space and the sidereal. In some credible theoretical circles, speculations of a hidden giant planet that manipulates orbits at the far reaches of our solar system still prevail. The Royal Astronomical Society not long ago spied no less than nine monster stars in the Tarantula Nebula, all nine of which outshine our sun by a factor of 30 million. Just a few weeks ago, several million miles closer to us, a supersonic parachute successfully blossomed from the NASA InSight Mars spacecraft, allowing this remote-controlled machine to land on Mars after falling at fireball velocities of over 12,000 miles per hour. The spacecraft, and those at mission control, have hatched plans to burrow into the red planet to inspect mysterious seismic activities some have labeled Martian earthquakes. Is the 21st century a setting fit for a cautionary 1950s Sci-Fi film like *The Thing from Another World*? Yes, unaccountably, it is.

A no less menacing weirdness pervades our lives on earth. Earthlings must brace ourselves against a long list of possible catastrophes in our voraciously bizarre corner of the universe. NASA's band of Nostradamuses have prognosticated a massive asteroid impact event as a possibility in 2135; this collision, it is forecast, would release the energy of several million nuclear weapons detonating simultaneously. Runaway scenarios of climate disruption may send us to colonize Mars, but today, the early stages of this phenomenon multiply ironies which are also living nightmares: Earthly wildfires have recently overtaken Paradise, California, and nearly two hundred endangered Ridley's Kemp Sea Turtles, lured to their doom by unseasonably warm climate disrupted waters, were recently found washed up on Cape Cod. Such tragedies should only anguish us in a fantastic story or poem, but our newborns are now born into just this threatening reality.

Here's some literary irony: The fantastic--an ancient genre around when Grendel first slithered into the Anglo-Saxon mead hall, and even earlier, when the forest ogre Humbaba cursed the tyrant king and his sasquatch-esque sidekick in *The Epic of Gilgamesh*, circa 1750 B.C.--may just be the most pertinent literary genre of all in the here and right now. Surely one might argue that the fantastic is best suited to imagine and express the whirlwind of violence we're doing in the Anthropocene, the destruction that we're doing to ourselves and other species in the process, and the unpredictable, spiraling repercussions. It is not the nature of the fantastic to shy away from the most improbable images captured by the Hubble Space Telescope, or from drones and autonomous vehicles, or from the rise of artifical intelligence. Maybe the fantastic can best frame the scary, hypothetical, precarious nature of our lives in the 21st century. And we may well require a fantastic imagination or two to create whatever will allow life on earth and earth itself to survive.

I suspect these are some of the reasons why our eighth and latest issue, *Hidden Planets, Monster Stars*, is such a veritable meteoroid of energy. This issue bears the stark birthmark of an earth umbilicaled to the Anthropocene, as well as to outer space and all that chaos. It's not at all surprising that falling cosmonauts close this issue, courtesy of Sonya Plenefisch, and that Jenny Grassl's "Making Grape Conserves" has "September" "cooking in the demon pot of suns." It's apt that, in Satoshi Iwai's "Pink-Active," the speaker's brother "has transformed into a three-legged flamingo living near the melted power plant," and quite fitting indeed that Harrison Demchick's ethereal mermaid hails from a tempting subterranean world known as "Magicland," where it is "never too hot." It's felicitous that, during Rick Krizman's tale, "little gods," "tiny lifeless faces with surprised looks" looked on "as the wind blew the grassfire back into the fields, and everything shushed."

We believe this eighth incarnation of *Phantom Drift* is a truly splendid issue. Thank you all for reading it, and thank you for contributing to this issue. Please spread the word. Join us in March at AWP in Portland. Happy holidays, Happy New Year, and happy travels in the unraveling multiverse.

Matt Schumacher
Managing Editor
Phantom Drift

TABLE OF CONTENTS

NON-FICTION/FEATURES

SATOSHI IWAI

PINK-ACTIVE

I receive an email from my brother who has transformed into a three-legged flamingo living near the melted power plant. He writes, "Wearing pink is the best way to sleep well in the immortal spring. While standing on one leg, I can use the other two legs to rub my itchy eyes."

Brother, my hay fever will never be cured, because our flowers never die until our land dies. Millions of cherry blossoms seem to be enjoying immortal hemophilia. They never stop dribbling tons of nectar. Our vaporized future is spreading in the warm wind.

My cellphone is about to die. His email begins to fade out: "It is so quiet here. I am so sleepy... ." Brother, you can write any ending to our dream with your third leg. Your feathers will become billions of pink pollen and contaminate the taciturn sea. Let's sleep, brother, like a sleeping fire.

 LINDA DOVE

TWO POEMS

FEAR IS A STICK-FIGURE MADE OF WOOD

It hangs out with trees
because it's hard to escape where it comes from.
It is looking at you,
the human, the heart
on the sleeve.
It doesn't use clothes as cover
because it has no use for charm.
At night, it is the legs on your bed.
In the day, it's the splinter in your thumb
that means you don't forget skin.
It doesn't let you forget.
Not totally.
It makes a brokenness
that doesn't know what to do with itself.
It is not just wood-bogged thumbs
anymore, it is eyes where tiny canoes live.
Not surprisingly,
it thinks of itself as potential.
It is skinny and liable to snap
in two like matches that line up
for their chance to burn.

FEAR IS A BIRD-VERB LIKE TO PARROT

It is the quick sleight of beak replacing lip, like a purse clasp that clicks shut
on a clutch of coins. It has a need to keep things from you.

It roosts in a large tree but not like a cartoon vulture because it is green
with wings that might be leaves. Every stem is a small branch.

It appears new that way. It looks relevant in its coat of green, which does not
stand for envy in this poem but maybe something more like survival.

It is a parrot that parrots. It prefers to reproduce itself, to collapse its lavender
feathers like a folded fan. It wants you to turn your nouns into verbs

so that your tongue is a bannister held by a firm hand. It is hard to see
what-is-what. It is quick. It takes away its chucks and whistles and hob-nobs

all at once in a sky slurry, which means there is a flock that lifts off in unison
or close to it. Nothing is as it seems against a backdrop of blue. It puts you on

defense or on-guard or in-a-nutshell because you are left on the ground,
staring up at its escape on a wing and a prayer, except you are the one

who's praying now. It hands you the verbs you need—*to parrot*, of course,
but also, *to swallow*, *to crow*, *to duck*. It wants you to believe that letters are not

in full molt, but then it adds *to owl* and *to egret*. And this is where
language starts to fail you. Its words get quiet in the dark like animals

when they sit on a branch under a branch and wait for the light or like ocean
in the trough of a wave. Across a fetch of open water, it is both a bird

and a verb, such as *to tern*. On land it is a thing that thrives among the trees,
to nuthatch down, *to creeper* up, where even *bark* sounds an alarm

out of a feral parrot that once lived with a dog. Now you take yourself
off the hook of language that wrote you into the forest as an oracle

because you are not an oracle, though you lie down on the forest floor.
In the morning inside the tree inside you is an unmade staircase.

HARRISON DEMCHICK

MAGICLAND

Duane is a boy who lives in a river. Or he lives in a house, that is, and the house is in a river, but this was not always the case. He thinks about this as he sits, arms wrapped around his knees, on the roof of his house in the river, looking across to the next house in the river, and the one behind it, and the one behind that. It's a muddy river, a deep brown with just a hint of sickly algae green. Mom tells him, has told him several times, not to go in the river, because *we need to stick together*. She has also told him not to call it a river. She said this very loudly.

Steven went in the river. That's how he got to Magicland.

The river used to be a road. It was a road about a week ago, although it's hard to tell, because the days are very long now, the big yellow sun beating down on the dull red tiles Duane had never seen from the roof before. He sweats as he sits up on the roof, and it should be a good thing that he lives in a river now, because he could go swimming to cool off, but Mom tells him no, even though there's not any air conditioning inside, and Dad tells Mom to shut the bad word up and stop babying Duane, and Parker is mean, and anyway it's still hot.

"Duane!" says Mom now from behind the window that opens onto the red-tiled roof. "Please."

Duane doesn't answer.

He looks out over the river. The river is still now, even with some envelopes and somebody's door floating in it. It wasn't still when it all came rushing in last week, alongside the fastest and heaviest storm Duane had ever seen, with wind that made the little trees in Mr. Gruber's front yard bend like gummy bears before breaking like pretzel logs and thunder and lightning that made the sky too bright to look at even at night. First the water was too shallow to be a river—more of a stream—but in only maybe an hour it was all the way up to the windows and rushing over the streets like white water rapids in West Virginia where Uncle Geoff (Dad's piece of bad word brother) took them one time last year when Duane was six. Duane and Parker and Mom and Dad were all sitting in the middle of the room downstairs, away from the windows, but Duane snuck over to the window by the smelly couch every now and then to see. They stayed down there until the river really became a river and started to become a river inside the house too, the carpet splashing like the swamp, and that's when they moved upstairs, which is where they all live now that their house is in a river forever.

Steven is way luckier. He doesn't have to live in a stupid upstairs and *stick together*. He gets to live in Magicland.

"Duane!"

Duane doesn't listen to Mom anymore, because Mom lied. Mom said Steven went to Heaven.

She told him this the morning after the rain stopped. That was a weird morning, because Duane hadn't had a good look at the river that used to be a street the day before, but now he could look out the window in his and Parker's (but mostly his) room upstairs and see water everywhere. But there were also a lot of people who weren't expecting there to be a river. They were floating, and very wet and kind of puffy. Parker said they were dead. Mom told him to be quiet. Dad told her to shut up. There were other things floating, like a dollhouse and the sign from the Taco Barn where they get tacos every Monday night except the third Monday because the third Monday is Dad's poker night and then Mom gets to choose and Mom doesn't really like Taco Barn.

Anyway, Mom was on the phone. Actually, Mom was on Dad's phone, using up all his bad word minutes. But Mom's phone had been downstairs, and downstairs was part of the river now. They were all in Mom and Dad's bedroom, which was sort of the new living room, even though there wasn't a table or anything more than some snacks and boxes of Nutty Os (instead of Honey Nut Cheerios because they are *not made of money*). And Mom was talking to someone, and she got a sad look on her face and said "I'm so sorry," the way grownups do when something bad happens, even when they don't have anything to do with it. And she turned off the phone, and Dad and Parker were playing a stupid card game with the weird cards with bad ladies on them, and she told Duane to come over and talk to her, and he did. And she said Steven had fallen into the river when the river was first becoming a river and it was raining very hard and the wind was blowing very hard too, and now he was in Heaven.

Duane knew what Heaven was because that's where Great Grandma Rosie went two years ago. It means someone is gone and you don't ever see them again. Duane decided to climb out the window and sit on the roof and look at the river and see if he could see Steven and that he wasn't really in Heaven. Mom held his arm as he was halfway out and told him not to, but Dad said to give the boy some space, and then Duane would have wanted to go and sit on the roof away from Mom and Dad and Parker anyway.

At first not much happened sitting on the roof, except for noticing the breaks in the red-tile pattern where some tiles had blown away. The river was quiet, except for the squawks of a few seagulls sitting in the water looking for fish. Duane wondered if there would be any fish in this river because it was a new river, or if fish would have to take their time finding the river. Maybe the seagulls were stupid for looking when there weren't any fish. Maybe the seagulls were smart and setting up a sinister trap for when the fish made it.

But then something cut through the water by the second house to the right across the street, where Skinny Todd lives. The water stirred and kicked up a bit like there was something right beneath. And Duane decided that there *was* a fish and the seagulls were smart after all.

Then, suddenly, a thick, scaly tail poked out of the water, reflecting a seaweed green in the bright afternoon sun, wet drops dripping off it and back into the river. The seagulls, startled, flapped their heavy wings and took fight, vanishing into the sky as the tail wiggled, wriggled, and disappeared.

Duane, wide-eyed, scooted up to the end of the roof so he could get a better look. His fingers dropped into the open space left by an absent tile. But the river water was too muddy to see anything underneath. The cawing of the seagulls faded into the distance, and Duane crept closer, closer, to the edge of the roof, which Duane could probably just barely reach from below if he were standing on the water on his tippy-toes. He stared at the water and held his breath and waited.

The tail appeared again, forked at the end, but not, Duane noticed, at the top and bottom like a fish, but on the sides like a manatee. It still looked like a fish tail though. And this time, as the tail fell below the water, something broke through the patch of water in front of it, rising up like a pyramid out of the desert. It wasn't a fish at all.

It was a lady.

"Hello," said the lady. She was a very pretty lady with smooth, dark skin and braids, and Duane would think she was a normal lady if he didn't know she had a giant green fish tail. She didn't have a bra and Duane could see *everything*.

Duane stared for a moment. Then, slowly, he said, "Are you a mermaid?"

"Yes, Duane," said the mermaid.

"You know my name?"

"Of course I know your name!" The mermaid giggled, bobbing up and down in the glistening river. "Steven sent me."

"Steven?"

"Of course!" Then the mermaid, grinning, shot upward, then curved, arcing perfectly into the water. Her fish tail curved up after her and disappeared below the surface just as her face emerged again. She bobbed up and she bobbed down, and she looked into Duane's wide-open eyes.

"Mom said Steven was in Heaven," said Duane.

"Oh, no, he's not in Heaven," said the mermaid. "There aren't any mermaids in Heaven. Steven is in Magicland."

"Magicland?" said Duane.

"Where else?"

Of course, Duane knew all about Magicland. In fact, it was Steven who told him about it, and Steven only knew because his cousin Paolo told him about it when they were on vacation in Fort Myers and everybody else but Steven's big sister Julie (who was listening to her iPod and wouldn't hear anything if the whole world exploded) had gone back to the room, so nobody could overhear. Only really special super-secret people knew about Magicland.

Magicland was a place underneath everywhere, like Kenner and Washington and even Canada, and you had to go down like twelve miles to find it, which is why it was hard to find. The best way to find it was to jump into a volcano, because even though volcanoes are really high up, they're the only place where you have a hole into the world that goes down for a while—even if not all the twelve miles, then enough that you can start digging. And you had to dig for hours, Steven said, chopping away at sedimentary and volcanic and igneous rock, and at first it would be very cold and very dark, but if you chopped and dug long enough, and if every now and then you put your ear to the rock and closed your eyes and didn't breathe and listened really really hard, you'd start to hear singing, and it would be the best and most awesome song ever written, and that's how you knew you were close to Magicland.

There was a password to get into Magicland. Steven didn't know what the password was, but he said you don't really have to know it, because people in Magicland have psychic powers, and they can tell just by looking at you whether or not you're a really special super-secret person who will protect the secret of Magicland. And once you were in, everything was amazing. They had chocolate that grew on chocolate trees, but it was a special kind of chocolate that was filled with vitamins and nutrients and healthy things that meant you could eat as much as you want and never feel sick or throw up. They had video games that were, like, fifty years ahead of any games back home, and you could walk in and be *inside* the game, and shoot things with your *mind*, and there was enough time for everybody to play as much as they wanted. And there were oceans and rivers filled with mermaids and mermen and dinosaur pirates, and you could play football and be amazing at it because everyone in Magicland is amazing at everything, and everyone was nice to everyone and no one yelled and told you to clean your room or get off the roof or go to bed or shut the bad word up.

Steven had never been there, but he said he really wanted to go. And Duane should come too.

Now, Duane lay on his stomach at the end of the roof and looked into the eyes of the pretty mermaid in the muddy river that was a street before yesterday happened.

"Mom said Steven went to Heaven," said Duane.

"She also said she was going to get you a pet snapping turtle," said the mermaid.

This was a good point.

"Why would she lie?" said Duane.

"She doesn't *want* you to go to Magicland," said the mermaid.

"I get to go?"

"All the really special super-secret people get to go," said the mermaid. "That's why Steven sent me. Come on, Duane!" She waved Duane toward the water, her smile brighter than the blinding, nonstop lightning from the night before, which flashed so fast Mom said somebody would have a seizure.

"But Mom said not to go in the river," said Duane. "She said we gotta stick together."

Instantly the mermaid's smile was gone. The sun seemed to fade a little with it, as her naked body bobbed up and down in the muddy brown and algae green water. "Hm," she said. She cocked her head to the right. "Maybe you're not really special super-secret after all." And with that, she hoisted herself up from the water, curved again, and sank down below as smoothly and perfectly as a rocket torpedo. The water didn't even splash, and she didn't come up again.

***

That was about a week ago. The second time Duane saw the mermaid was a few days after. Mom cried a lot in those days. She sat in the corner of the bedroom, underneath the powerless turquoise lamp with the base that cracked when Duane and Parker were fighting on the bed last year (and they were both punished for it even though Parker started it, and with the rubber cement you can't even see it was cracked), and she cried, most of the time for no good bad word reason at all, Dad said. Her eyes were red and he yelled, and Parker ate all the Doritos when they hardly had any to begin with, and no one seemed to care that Steven was in Magicland.

Maybe Mom felt guilty for lying. Maybe she just made a mistake, or maybe Steven's parents really told her Steven was in Heaven. After all, most people didn't know about Magicland. Steven had told him that Paolo specifically said grownups usually don't know, because only kids get to go, and it's not like Mom could call back and find out if Steven's parents heard any different because the phone was dead. Or maybe she was crying because she hurt something, like when Duane stepped on a piece of glass from a shattered cup in the kitchen and didn't say anything because he wanted to be tough, but Mom saw him crying and made him go to the hospital where they put a needle in his arm, even though the glass had been in his foot. (The kitchen was all underwater now.)

Duane tried to ask Mom why she was crying. She didn't say why. She just said Duane had to be strong for her, whatever that meant. Dad said for her to stop her bad word crying. It was very crowded upstairs, the kind of crowded where your skin feels sharp and one hundred degrees, and you scratch at it and scratch but there's no air and the hotness doesn't go away. Duane wanted to go to his room and play *Plants vs. Zombies* but he couldn't, because there was no electricity and electricity is what makes all the good things work. He couldn't even go to his room and read a book and be alone because Parker was in there, grounded for eating too much of all the food there even was and not sharing with everybody else, as if they didn't have *enough* problems.

Mom cried, and Dad coiled, and Duane opened the window and walked back out onto the roof, where he'd gone for a few minutes every day to look for the mermaid.

It was only a little hotter outside than it was inside, and sometimes there was a breeze off the river that made it seem cooler. The breeze was invisible, but you could see it sometimes if you looked at the river, because a tiny V would cut through the rolling water like an invisible flock of birds. Sometimes Duane imagined that there *were* birds underneath. Sometimes Duane wanted to roll into the water and see for himself.

Today he sat curled, his knees pulled into his chest by his clasped arms, and he wondered if it was Monday or Tuesday or no day at all. A basketball floated on the water. A science test floated on the water. A skinny girl floated on the water. Duane didn't feel very well, so he looked up into the sky, where a thin wisp of a cloud passed, but nowhere near the sun, and that's the only cloud there was.

A low plop directed Duane's eyes back toward the rolling river. A few stray bubbles rose to the surface, just barely missing a square black board that maybe used to be a table. Another gust of wind carried an invisible flock across the water, until the V was broken into a million pieces by the forked tip of a fish tail.

Duane smiled.

With the grace of a dolphin or a superhero, the mermaid rose out of the water, droplets dripping slowly down her ropelike braids. She shook her head left and right, and a drizzle came off her, feeding the body of water she lived in. She looked up at Duane and she smiled, and when she smiled all the sharp and the heat floated and fluttered away.

"Hi," said Duane.

"Hi, Duane," said the mermaid.

"You came back."

"Steven asked me to come back," the mermaid said, bobbing in the water like a buoy. "He said that Magicland isn't really Magicland without Duane."

"He did?" said Duane.

"He said he's saving a place in Magicland just for you."

Slowly, Duane pulled his arms apart. He crouched to his knees, then lay forward, his head dangling over the end of the roof. He was closer to the mermaid now—so close that maybe, if he stretched out and reached as far as the tiniest tips of his fingers could reach, and if she did the same, maybe they could touch, and he'd be the first kid in, like, the universe to touch a mermaid, except probably for Steven.

"How did Steven get there?" said Duane. "I thought Magicland was at the bottom of a volcano."

"There are other ways to get to Magicland," said the mermaid. "Do you wanna know a secret?"

Eyes wide, Duane nodded.

"There's no street underneath this river," said the mermaid. "Not anymore. It used to be a street, but now it's just water, all the way down. If you hold your breath and jump in and keep swimming, and swim and swim and swim until you can't hold your breath, and then keep swimming even longer, you'll make it to Magicland."

"That's how Steven got there?"

"Yes," said the mermaid. "Steven was the only boy brave enough to swim all the way down to Magicland. But he said if there's anyone else who's brave enough and strong enough to swim down to Magicland, it's Duane."

Duane looked past the mermaid down toward the water. He remembered the street that used to be underneath it, with the loose gravel you could kick really far if you had the right shoes and all the potholes a block down the road the bad word government had to get off its bad word and do something about. But the river was murky and Duane couldn't see anything below it, not even the mermaid's tail, even though it had to be right near the top. He tried to imagine a river so deep it went on nearly forever and found it hard to fit it all into his head.

"Mom said to stop calling it a river," said Duane. "She said it's a street."

"I'll bet she told you not to swim in it either," said the mermaid.

"Yeah," said Duane.

"Know why? Because she knows that if you swam in the water, you'd make it to Magicland, and she doesn't want you to go to Magicland."

"Why not?"

"Because she's mean," said the mermaid. "She needs to shut the bad word up."

Duane felt a tightness under his stomach, as if his body didn't know whether to cough or sneeze or throw up and decided instead to stop just short of doing anything. But his fingers did grip the edge of the roof, very very tightly.

"She doesn't mean to be," he said quietly.

The mermaid didn't say anything. She just bobbed and bobbed and bobbed.

"Is it hot in Magicland?" said Duane.

"It's never too hot in Magicland," said the mermaid. "You can wear shorts all the time, but you never have to go inside."

"Is there food in Magicland?" said Duane.

"Whatever you want."

Duane glanced back toward the window. "But Mom said I had to be strong for her. I think I'm not supposed to go away." He turned back toward the mermaid. "Can I take them with me? Can they go too?"

"Why should they get to go to Magicland?" said the mermaid, suddenly cross. "Why does Magicland need a big brother who eats all the Doritos and doesn't even share one? Why does Magicland need a dad who's mean and angry and yells? Why does Magicland need a mom who's always crying and lying and telling you what to do?"

"But they wouldn't be like that if I told them!" said Duane. "I could tell them to be on their very best behavior. And Mom wouldn't cry if there was a lot of food. Dad wouldn't yell if everything was nice all the time. And Parker could find other kids his age and not bother me anymore." He pushed his head further out off the roof. "They'd be happy 'cause I *helped* them! And made everything *better*!"

Duane turned to the window behind him. "You'll see. I can do it! I can—"

But when he looked back toward the river, the mermaid was gone. He hadn't even heard a splash.

Duane sat outside for another hour after that, until Mom, her face flushed and puffy, came to the window and told him to go inside.

The mermaid did not return.

***

Duane is a boy who lives in a river. He sits on the rooftop as the sun behind him starts to sink into the horizon, underneath its own river, and he ignores Mom's voice begging him, please, to come inside.

He told them about Magicland. Of course. He had to. They had to *stick together*. He had to *be strong* for her. For them. And if Steven didn't have to live upstairs, where the food is now two days gone, and if Steven didn't have to bake in an oven inside or roast under the sun outside, and if Steven was allowed to dive into the river and reappear in a place with chocolate trees and video games and dinosaur pirates, then why couldn't they?

So he told them a few days ago, as Dad scoured the attic for old cans of stupid beans. And he told them yesterday, as Mom looked out the window for a helicopter. And when Dad tore the covers off the bed and threw the lamp against the wall and broke it in so many places all the king's rubber cement couldn't put it back together again, when he hollered and shouted and kicked and yelled, Duane told them again that they could get away and *stick together* and *be strong* if they went into the sun and held their breath and jumped into the river and kept swimming, and swam and swam and swam until they couldn't hold their breath, and then kept swimming even longer, until they found their way to Magicland.

And Dad turned, and his eyes got real small, and he turned and he tensed and he yelled that *there is no Magicland* and *Steven isn't in Magicland* and *Steven is dead dead dead DEAD DEAD DEAD*—

It's almost dark now. Mom isn't yelling anymore. She shut the bad word up.

A low plop emerges from the river. Duane turns his tired eyes toward it.

The mermaid surfaces. She doesn't look so bright with the sun nearly gone, but he can still see her smile.

Duane feels that feeling again. Like his body wants to do everything at once. Like he could swim in all directions until there's nothing left of him.

"I want to go to Magicland," he says. It's almost a whisper. He looks into the eyes of the mermaid. "Can I still go? Can you still take me to Magicland?"

With a light trickle of water, the mermaid swims just a few inches closer. "Of course," she says, softly. "You're special super-secret, aren't you?"

He is.

So Duane looks around him: at the tiles on the roof, at Mr. Gruber's house across the street he can hardly see anymore, at the last orange cloud in the sky. But not at the window behind him. Never there. He waits for a moment, then takes the biggest, most super-amazing breath anyone has ever taken, so he can hold more air than anyone ever has before.

The mermaid pushes herself back a few feet to give him room.

Hands pressed against one another as if in prayer, Duane rocks back, then forth, then back again. Then he pushes ahead, leans forward, and dives into the river, and swims and swims and swims until he can't hold his breath anymore.

Memory Box

 DEVON BALWIT

THE FOURTH YEAR

*If a man be in debt, and sell his wife, his son, or his daughter for the money, or
has handed them over to service for three years they shall work in the house
of their purchaser or exploiter; in the fourth year they shall be set at liberty.*
(The Code of Hammurabi)

I know what it says, the words read to me,
shackled and shuffled off to shell beans,

to sweep and to serve, handed over,
like a tethered goat, teats for the pulling,

and, in nine months, another man's kid
dropped in straw, a bonus-babe.

Emptied from one house, I furnish another,
its mistress eying me askance at as if I chose

to haul water, to scrub on my knees, to be
taken here by the master, his sweat

second-skinning me with a scurf of dust.
Sometimes across the road, lurking in shadow,

I glimpse the one who offered me up.
Is he missing me or the ease of me?

I'll never know. Marking each day
in a secret tally, come the fourth year,

bond paid and gate slipped open,
I'll not return to either.

CAROLINE PLASKET

AS IF WE ARE

Your face in my neck,
asleep there, the velvet
breath moving out of you like bell chimes
tucking their chant into my hair,
like the moss the bird sews
into its home. I am your *sulde*—your spirit
banner. There is an exchange
in our sleep, a sermon
of pheromones. A bartering
of cells landing, me to you, you to me,
skin to be read like periodicals.
A bazaar of scent, your oils are something
my sleeping self senses, it stores vials of,
to memorize as though there is
an internal chemist alive inside of me,
not so unlike the little person
I thought lived in the radio,
when I was a child, singing and playing
in their little bandstand. Blasting it
through the little holes. It was such
a depression to learn it was all just
plastic and wires. My little friend
wasn't there waiting for my summons
but came through some other enigma
where sound surfs the air and studied itself
into the Sony machine. As a girl I wanted
a mirror so I could see
the body I would one day marry
and I knew even then he had

olive skin and dark hair. As if the little
chemist told me about the apothecary
they were readying for later as if we have
always been in this sleep state, buried
in one another as if we are
the egg and the sperm as if we are
a movement into some eternal unity.

 JAMES GRABILL

A FEW STEPS OUT THE DOOR

Where there's a door, should there be a key? It isn't a problem until Pavlov's doorbell rings. It could never depend on hectares of western Roosevelt forests with trust-busting photosynthetic devices, until it certainly does.

The present couldn't know the meaning of lonely, not when the future is already always visiting with its bag of tropical nuts.

Doesn't the present already know more than enough, more than anyone could keep up with? Doesn't the present have its hands full, where being intact inculcates not only hemoglobin production, but the long-time shock of consciousness to the autonomous systems?

Haven't bison-blooded bonds cried in rooms of birth? Through winds ladling overhead waters, doesn't the compulsive naming of things after people tie up urban phone lines?

Of course, everyone goes back to the same inscrutable mother whose effects quicken in the undone as in the done. So the Wild West willingness to sacrifice beauty in the name of utility originated with whom?

When magical wishing calls back from the horizon, *You still need me there?*, the galaxy's spiraling in space, flaming out of its atoms through suns. Its pulses endow seeds along spiral arcs on the face of a sunflower with dark rooms and flames of suns not in suns but cells.

DONNA PRINZMETAL

SPECTER

Don't even think about ignoring me.
In the albino light
I've been puncturing the black bubble
you call home.
It's not enough to light candles,
to clutch the clear quartz to your heart
listen to old songs that remind you of what?
It's time to ask what haunts you,
that's right, I said it.
You want it to be beautiful:
belladonna sunsets,
the scent of lilacs,
not some homunculus trying to stay on a bucking bronco
or how wax bears the handprint
of all the held hands, not just the good ones,
but the pockmarked wart ridden skin
you hated to touch.
The shed with its spider web wisps
and musty smell.
All the mumbo jumbo that was said to you
and that you said.
In the aftermath of gloom
more gloom.
You don't want to see me with my disheveled kelp hair
my overalls and stay awake silences.
Let me tell you something,
you can leave the lights on all night,
get a dog,

huddle in the corner with a full box of tissue
watching a Hallmark special.
It won't matter.
Your arm still holds the white ghosts of fingerprints
where you were grabbed.
The ransacked house is still there.
And me, I'm over here smoking a pack of Luckies
because it doesn't matter any more.
You with your redacted life
looking for evidence the past even existed,
while I've got all the time in the world.

JOSHUA MCKINNEY

THE AFFAIR

You sit down at your desk, stare at the blank pages and move in under the shadow of trees. They are oaks you think. A trail leads into a wood and you follow it, winding down slope to a creek where dark water halts your progress. At dinner, your wife is quiet. She cuts her steak, nudges the pieces around her plate with the tip of her knife. She is still reading to the children when you go to bed, and in the morning she appears to be asleep when you rise in the dark and dress for work. In the evening

you sit down at your desk. The trees are not oaks after all; they are pines and you wonder how you didn't see this before. You didn't see the rocks, either, the ones that now allow you to hop across the creek to where the trail resumes. You follow it up the bank and soon it intersects a dirt road, flanked by fields of tall green corn. The road runs straight for half a mile, and in the distance you can make out some structure, perhaps a small house. You hear voices coming out of the field, calling for you to come and tuck them in. Later, in bed, your wife rolls over, away from you, leaving a space in which crows circle above rows of tall corn. In the morning

she is waiting for you at the kitchen table, her saucer full of cigarette butts, her coffee cup steaming rings in the table top. She says you have been seen entering a house without electricity, a house of clapboard and tin at the end of a long dirt road. She asks what you have to say for yourself. There is denial, of course, and yelling and perhaps some broken dishes though the crashing is distant as you retreat to your study and call in sick to work. You leave your drafts on your desk with your wife's cigarette lighter as a paperweight and go out to the backyard with a notebook and a pen. You sit in the deckchair,

step in under the pines and stride down the trail. Someone has laid planks over the creek, and as you hurry across you feel them flex beneath your feet. When you reach the road you make for the house in the distance. It's a house, you can see that now, though some might call it a shack. Its tin roof flashes in the sun like some shiny thing a crow might covet. The morning sun is warm and you are sweating freely as you notice the corn is now withered and dry, the stalks and tassels so blond they seem themselves to emit light. A breeze rises at your back, nudging you toward the house where a woman is hanging laundry in the side yard on a line strung between two locust trees. It's then you smell smoke.

Turning, you see the fields are on fire, the flames moving toward you with a terrible urgency. You break into a run. Up ahead, the front door of the house is open and now the woman stands before it in a cotton sundress with a pattern of small pink roses, though perhaps you are still too far away to see clearly. You feel the heat from the flames at your back. Your lungs burn and your legs are heavy from lack of oxygen. The woman stands in the doorway now, her long hair black as a crow's wing, and you can see the silhouette of her bare thighs through her dress. You must reach her. Has anything ever mattered this much? You kick hard as she turns and disappears inside, leaving the door open. Small embers and bits of burning chaff fill the air and smoke burns your eyes and throat. You know that, somehow, you must get inside the house, and you know that even if you do it all must be consumed.

Brittney Corrigan

TWO POEMS

TATTOO ARTIST'S DAUGHTER

I'm not afraid of needles or blood.
I have watched skulls revealed,
seen snakes wind glistening on
human limbs, looked ghost faces
full in the eyes, witnessed dragons
rise up with their leathery wings.

I have read messages chiseled into
delicate skin, the script still weeping
sanguine droplets from kays and wys
and ars. Cyrillic, cuneiform, kanji.
Pictographs, hieroglyphs, runes. The needle
a cipher of every alphabet and tongue.

I have seen birds take flight across
women's breasts, trailing feathers
and seeds. Open-mouthed lions and bears
rippling on shoulders and pecs. Tentacled
beasts, mercreatures with filigreed fins,
surfacing on quivering bellies and thighs.

Holes where there are no holes. Wings
that imagine flight. Flowers that grow
and bloom and wither in the soil
of flesh, in sweat-sweet rain. Anchors

with no sea to salt them, knives and swords
that will never split open any solid thing.

Names of the lost, the beloved. Mosaics
of pattern and shape. Tessellations
nesting as the inky needle hums. Cities
rise up. Trees and bridges and stones
sprawl across trembling backs as outline
turns to fill and the colors drone.

Here are my wrists, my fingers. Palms
and ankles, calves and shins. My shoulder
blades and arms, my chest and thighs.
My collarbone, my neck, my hands and feet.
Belly and back. Body you created and named.
Child of tabula rasa. Child of entreated pain.

WEREWOLF'S DAUGHTER

You never hear about the girls,
though we are the ones at peace
with the moon and its pull upon
our bodies, our bellies brimming
with lunar light, the way it bends
us, turns our insides out.

Howling at the moon feels like
doubling in size, shoulder muscles
triangulating, throat opening, calling
down stars. The power to raise
gooseflesh, petrify motion,
stand every last hair on end.

Fur growing like a time-lapse
garden, a thickening mammalian
boon. Pelt of shadowed hues, dense
and warm and shaggy with musk.
Snout lengthening into ripened flares.
Dervish of tail and teeth and claws.

Father fights every turning, writhing
in his lupusing skin. It's just like
you imagine it: shredding his workshirt,
pawing at the rising topography of his skin,
moaning and keening and bawling into
the darkness as he sprints for the trees.

But it's a beautiful thing, the morphing.
I shift in the water to dull the pain, naked
and cold and the raucous frogs silencing

with awe. My bones spin and incandesce,
each nail sharpens and curves, blue
eyes wax yellow and gleam.

A girl-wolf will rise and shake moonwater
from her body not like a dog, but like
a gorgeous beast, every small creature
retreating before the heat of her heart.
A girl-wolf will rock back on her sinewy
haunches to thank the benevolent moon.

F. Daniel Rzicznek

from LEAFMOLD

And down to the hovercraft. Breton and Èluard lace up their store-new boots and double back toward the landing strip. A lady went under the train. A lady came out of the lady. The travelers spindled their programs. A lobster shouted *asshole rhymes with castle*. A falling out with the good shepherd. A dude went under the train and emerged flanked by a battalion of phantom children, their liquid tails wriggling. Then came a year of perpetual flu—junk mail piling in drifts among the doors, threats issued by no one to nobody as birds and small animals did their best to survive in the negative-thirteen nights. A question sewn from noontime cloth, the very next paragraph vomiting a waterfall of hand-me-downs. Consistency of argument never lasts. Her middle name was *snow*. Little sister to famine, most painful love you can know, hard as the road you walked here, the same road snaking home. Strap on your vegan sneakers and beat it. No, come back. I excel at frightening myself with opulence. Two inches of wet snow through dawn. Each swipe of the shovel brings you closer to an unattainable cleanliness. Who has more pixels? If we really ask, the sky turns away, blushing.

 ALEXCINTRON

FOR ONE NIGHT ONLY:
ACT TWO (PARTIAL)

a well. torrent. at the base of the great pyramid. the ancient pool.
down the corridor of time, world continues to spin, its bell rings.
the universe deployed to keep secret the cosmic convoy.

the grave of robinson jeffers.
sunflower blossoms haunting the coast line with their midnight eyes.
a landscape without end.

buried in the eyes of marianne moore, metallic teeth shining in the sunlight
eyes buried in the downpour where no one lives
a cave hidden in the white isle, cliffs crowing when found murder
i wear the face of the spider when its asleep
too well have tomorrows spent money and time searching their own birth
an island! one's destiny following the ravine
...talk about silence. a murder!

where statues of planets come face to face with their sculptor
an alchemic elegy
no road too neat to snow
i hate to admit it, but this island is surrounded by water...
— is that supposed to happen?
no one left to forget

caught the left from a blind side

my drink turning into swan

i scrape the shadow out from my eyelids
        rolling blossoms with their own petals
               — ripe to smoke
     bodies lay on backs of white serpents
     my favorite source of wealth
             how often do you actually iron your clothes?
        fold the grave up like an origami moon
               i am my own metal fish!

Mind Travels

 Rick Krizman

LITTLE GODS

The gods parachute down from the sky; thousands of them breezing across the Mojave like dandelion spores, tiny and manlike, waving and calling out to each other in helium voices. They tumbleweed through the scrub, their chutes snagging on Joshua trees and tinder-dry sagebrush. Barely six inches tall, they carry backpacks almost as big as them, and now they pull out rods and wheels and little wrenches and assemble tiny cars with oversized tires, perfect for the rough desert floor, and before you know it they are speeding off in all directions, some bumping along the shoulder of Route 14 towards the mountains, others heading south to what's left of Los Angeles.

Maybe we'd been expecting the Overlords, or the thundering gods of Asgar, or even the God-Father of Christianity, the white-bearded Big Guy himself, when we heard our prayers had been answered. Not that anybody thought we had a nickel's worth of future left, what with the radiation wars, Miami and Manhattan under water, the flip of the magnetic poles, the generations of mutations that—well, who knew the Van Allen belt was anything more than a Wikipedia entry? And anybody can make that shit up.

But at least we had the Seeds, maybe the last ones, and now even better, these gods, one for every trailer. I knew Ruth was jealous of Elizabeth's little guy, who could play a toy piano and sing show tunes in his chirpy voice, but I figured we were lucky to have one at all. He had a name, which sounded like you're stuttering when you say it, some of the frequencies we can't hear apparently, so we just called him Rodney, and he seemed to like that.

Ruth and I'd never had kids, because why risk finding out you got the horn-head gene and get shamed out of the Trailer Utopia and have to live across the creek bed with people who were forced to pretend that a rhinoceros horn sticking out of your forehead was...well, point being, what did we know about parenting, so it was iffy at first, like when Rodney almost got eaten by Rooster Dave (who himself we will soon see at the dinner table). He liked to poke around in dark places, like the bathtub drain, or the underside of the Franklin stove, and it was always on the list to make sure he wasn't washed away or accidentally cooked on a cold day when we were burning the last bits of the House Next

Door. "Where's Rodney?" was the thing we always asked before emptying the waste can or letting Big Kitty out of her room in the morning.

Elizabeth and Shirley discovered their gods were twins, and often dressed them alike and pushed them around the co-op in the front of their cart. Vivian's little man wrote French poetry, and sometimes she'd bring him over where he'd recite his newest poems, which we didn't have to understand to know they were beautiful because of the rolling words. Ed took it on to organize soccer games on Saturday mornings, and we'd line either side of the dirt behind his trailer and cheer on our tiny charges, who were kicking around a ping-pong ball, yipping and elbowing each other like they were having a complete blast. But our Rodney didn't so much enjoy playing with the other gods, and would prefer to stay home with Ruth, perched on the kitchen counter where Big Kitty couldn't go, watching her boil the bones, or he'd just gaze out the window, full of mysterious godly thoughts probably. Sometimes I'd take him foraging, where he'd ride in my coat pocket and peer through the woods like a magpie, pointing out shiny things that only his tiny eyes could see. One day we found a sun-faded Fisher-Price dollhouse, one of those plastic ones that you couldn't destroy with the world's biggest sledgehammer, and Ruth set it up in the closet, where sometimes late at night we'd watch him sleep, listening to his squeaky little snores and trying to feel thankful for his small presence.

Every Sunday night the little gods drove their toy cars down to the VFW, the old meeting place still left over from when there were soldiers to come back from the wars. You could stand outside and hear their pipsqueak voices, sometimes music, maybe just xylophone and bongo drums, and smell roasting meats and strange smoke. We'd watch them come out, long after midnight, staggering arm in arm toward their little cars, then zig-zagging woozily down the dirt tracks to their homes. We left them alone, like this was probably their night to commune with their own kind, without having to be...well, whatever they were being for us, which as far as gods go, was, to be honest, not much.

But still, with the gods just being here things didn't seem so bad; not exactly life is grand, but we counted our blessings and number one was our Trailer Park itself, well-tucked into the trees, but close enough to the remains of the world so we could scrape by, separated from the horn-head Down-and-Overs by the creek bed No-Man's-Land. Maybe we were kidding ourselves about the tin trailer walls blocking the Gammas, but still, it could be; after all, who would've sent the little gods if it was all just a Hot Radioactive Mess?

But the thing that was not on our list of blessings was there was never enough Good Food. Ruth wasn't looking too healthy, bone-thin and her cough rattling almost all the time. Ed behind us had the Seeds, of course, but the rocky woods on our side of the creek bed didn't offer much hope, and there was no talking to those Down-and-Over hornheads who had all the rich black earth, but what did they think, that they'd just have an immaculate conception of corn?

One particularly cold night the three of us—Ruth, Rodney, and me—were scrunched up to the stove, making the most of some scraps of sappy pine, getting more smoke than heat, when Ruth started coughing her head off, worse than usual, this on top of her yellowing skin, and the clumps of hair I'd seen in the sink, and I looked at Rodney, wanting to say, What good is it having a god—but then Ruth coughed again like she had a knife in her throat and Rodney gave a soft whistle, as if to say What can I do?

I told Rodney, I know you're a god, not a farmer. But there was a guy once, one of the Old Gods, who could just reach out his hand...I shut my eyes and placed a palm on Ruth's forehead, like to demonstrate. Then when I looked, Rodney had pulled himself up onto Ruth and was curled into her lap. She stroked his little head of doll-like curls, and for whatever reason her cough went quiet and her eyelids drooped. I covered them both up with the army blanket and fed another piece of siding into the Franklin.

Then was the morning with Ed banging on my door before the sun was up. The Seeds are gone, he said when I opened it. All three bags? Yup, disappeared. I saw Rodney poke his head out of the second floor of the dollhouse, then heard tiny steps as he hurried down the stairs and flapped out the kitty door, and before we knew it Ed and I could see him through the window in his little car bumping down the sidewalk toward the VFW. A few more revved up behind him—Is that your guy? I asked Ed, who nodded and scratched his head—and I must have counted a couple dozen as they rounded the corner.

Where are they going? It was Sue, Ed's wife. I stepped out onto the gravel to where I could see people coming out of trailers, not knowing what's up.

The Seeds, they're gone, Ed shouted down the way, then everyone was out in the yard talking all at once, about who might have taken them. Was it the little gods? The Down-and-Overs? Maybe a traitor, right here? At that idea everybody shut up and looked at each other.

My wife is sick, I said, but I'd never—

No need for that, Ed said, putting a hand on my shoulder. It was them bastard horn-heads, likely got their gods to sneak those seeds away while I was sleeping like a baby, when I should have been—

He couldn't go on, and I patted his hand. Don't worry Ed, we'll find them and get them back.

Well, where the hell did they get off to, yelled Vivian, and everybody said some version of Yeah, then of course we all started down toward the VFW.

We saw all their little cars abandoned on the sidewalk. We could smell smoke and something like burning rubber, heard scratching, clanking sounds from inside, and voices chanting something in their stuttering way. Ed walked towards the service door but it flew open and there were our little gods, scores of them, dressed in blue jumpsuits and black helmets, shouldering pint-sized rifles, marching out in two straight columns behind a little god drummer, stepping in time and shouting out on every fourth step, heading straight for the creek bed. Behind them a line of whining, scale-model tanks towed observation balloons that hung six or seven feet in the air, with their god-gondoliers glassing the fields across the creek. I hardly recognized Rodney, up near the front, gripping his rifle butt and staring straight ahead. We all stood, stunned, watching the parade inch past us. Ed next to me even saluted. Go with god, I heard him whisper, and I'm not a crier, but still, I almost did.

We fell back into the trees and followed our troops along the No-Man's creek bed until we heard chanting coming from the other side, and saw balloons peeking above the deep grass that had overtaken the Rich Black Earth of the Down-and-Overs. Then the weeds parted and a stream of little gods in red jumpsuits with shiny white helmets spilled out, followed by their own tanks, and lined up along the opposite side of the creek bed as our own soldiers were lining up on ours. The drums stopped, then a puny voice cried out and the front rows dropped to one knee, and two lines of rifles pointed at each other across the dry cobble. Ruth squeezed my arm—No, no, no, no, she whispered, just before the creek bed exploded with the popping of a thousand cap pistols, puffing out a smoky haze, followed by ungodly squealing sounds that could only be the gods themselves. Through the cloud we could see blue- and red-clad bodies falling and twitching like broken toys, while the remaining soldiers lined up again, more cap guns exploded and the sound of bottle rockets sizzled from the tanks, then flashes everywhere, smoking up the trees and catching fire to the grass, and as the flames jumped up to the balloons we heard yelping and saw the little gods leap from their baskets. Then all the ones left let out a banshee cry and rushed at each other, stabbing with their bayonets as the tanks fired away, the grass fire building, until there was nothing we could see, standing in the trees and listening to their squeaky cries. My eyes stung and I felt sick from an awful smell. Ed next to me retched up, and Ruth squeezed my arm tighter than ever.

The whole thing couldn't have been more than five minutes. The wind turned and blew the grass fire back into the fields, and everything shushed. We came out from our trees, looking for anything moving but only seeing twisted bodies, tiny lifeless faces with surprised looks, legs and arms, and even heads, strewn about like a spilled bucket of doll parts. A Down-and-Over woman, with the biggest horn I'd ever seen up close, broke into tears as she picked up a tiny rag doll and clutched it to her breast, then hurried away through her charred field. Ruth waited in the trees while I looked for Rodney, finding him face down in the middle of the creek bed. I turned him over, shocked to see the blood still leaking from where a bullet had blown right through his heart.

The trailers were mostly quiet that night, with only dim lights glowing in the windows. You could hear someone crying across the way, and some kind of mournful singing here and there. Ruth had cleaned up Rodney as best she could, dressed him in the neat blue suit he'd worn the day he arrived, and laid him out on his little bed. Tomorrow would be soon enough to dig the hole in the back yard.

The next morning I had the same thought as everyone else, apparently, when we all found ourselves walking to the VFW, where the little cars still waited for their never-to-return drivers. We stepped through the unlocked door, first noticing the benches full of tools, the miniature die-casting machinery, coffee cups full of tank parts, bayonets, a helium tank, and other scale-model war-bent bits and pieces scattered around the assembly-room floor, then, in the corner of the room we saw Ed's three bags of Seeds.

Them sons of bitches, Ed said.

They stole them? someone offered.

I bet to keep an eye on them, I said, but not so sure.

Everyone began talking all at once, when behind us the door opened, and we turned to see a group of Down-and-Overs standing there. The room went quiet and I looked for something to use as a weapon, but only saw toothpick-size sabers and some lady-finger firecrackers. Ed took a step toward them, but the one in front, who had the biggest horn, raised his hands and faced his palms toward us, then stepped to one side and a woman—

or maybe a young girl because she only had a small, rounded nub in her forehead, more pretty than I thought a horn-head could be—carried a little canvas bag to the center of the room. She upended it, and you could smell the black dirt that spilled out into a pile on the floor. Before Ed could even say anything Elizabeth was already going for the Seeds. I put one arm around Ruth; she turned her head into my neck and began to sob quietly.

***

Meanwhile, witnesses in Belgium report seeing thousands of tiny men hanging from paper airplanes, gliding in across the chlorine-bleached fields of Flanders...

 DAN FROST

AND SO

We grew restless, and so
went to live for a time
in a small, ruined republic
on the earth's equator.

A witch blessed our yellow house
and told us it was the mother
with breath and heartbeat.
Red spiders came at dusk
from banana trees in the courtyard
onto the terra cotta floor
where we could see the candlelight
in their small, big refractive eyes.

We drank cheap mescal at low tables
deep into the night
with strange friends.
The mescal tasted of soil and old saddle leather.
The women wore long earrings and
exhaled slowly from thin cigarettes
as they told sad, dark stories

of their fathers' mistresses
and unknown half-sisters.
The men would lean back
into the cushions with closed eyes,
to murmur comments of
lost lovers and places that did not exist
in soft, accented voices
we could not understand.

At the edge of the light
a solemn leopard tortoise
moved through the grass
to his own deliberate rhythm
in his own geometric shell.
Above him,
a white plaster angel
with arched back and heavy wings,
lit unevenly by our votives,
stood at the edge of the fountain
looking outward—
at what, we could never tell.
Together, the two bent memory and time
to their own purposes.
Sometimes, before dawn
we would hear notes like thunder.
Then we would climb the tiled stairs
to the balcony
and watch volcanoes
shoot great gouts
of orange sparks upward
at the rising sun.

Jonathan Greenhause

TWO POEMS

JEREMY ATTRACTS A FLURRY OF CONSTELLATIONS,

stars spinning 'round his waist like crazed moths flammable
& setting off sparks,

                    freely attaching themselves

to his pants' loose threads. He names their shifting conglomeration,

their mundane semblance to household items, baptizes them
"Bent Screwdriver",

                    "Crumpled-up inspirational poster", &

"Midnight sun over fjords." Despite this associated brilliance,

Jeremy's closest friends steer clear of him, are afraid to be present
in case of a supernova

                    despite his vague scientific assurances

that millions of years will pass before their disastrous expansion.

Diminutive clouds float right within his apartment, dense patches
of ice-cold condensation

                    causing a constant parade

of sunrises & sunsets. By the puddles beneath them,

Jeremy unfolds yellow easels warning "Caution: Wet floor,"
gently pats them dry
>   with the heat of a handheld sun.

His constellations don't appear to bother anyone, receive visits

from local fire departments, from the admiration of The Society
of American Astronomers
>   & a struggling community college

starting a brief course about solar systems inconceivably stuck

in the crowded layout of a studio apartment. Jeremy recognizes
the drawbacks, how his wife's
>   hesitant with his attempts at intimacy,

his patchwork of stars searing her cratered skin, celestial tattoos

painfully marking his clumsy efforts at love, at conjugation.
As Penelope undresses,
>   she's painstakingly gentle, is careful

not to knock his revolutionary suns off their wobbly trajectories

as she removes her garments in a rhythmic manner not upsetting
her own panoply of moons
>   spinning in their feeble gravity,

enamored around a bare midriff & illuminating her lunar eyes

with the slanted reflection of Jeremy's starred enchantment,
with his universal acceptance
>   of the mystery of space's vastness.

EAGER TO DIVE INTO THE REAL ESTATE MARKET,

Francisco builds a house within himself but must make room
for the crossing of beams,
                                        the utter gutting of structure,
the removal of organs & arteries.   He hires a foreperson,
gets construction underway,

trucks in paperless day-workers   who'll work below minimum wage.
He acquires his materials
                                        from mom-&-pop-killing chains,
& what he can't purchase   he salvages from people gone astray,
from dreams half-finished

auctioning off broken hearts   & lungs barely breathing.
Francisco engineers a staircase
                                        from his hipbone to neck
& a pole down each limb   empties into a 4-post bed.
He crafts a swimming pool

floating by his abdomen,   has a plumber lay down pipe
directly along his groin
                                        to facilitate proper drainage
so as to avoid a regrettable mess,   & he hires an electrician
to string up the circuitry

so he'll be ready to plug in.   Once the framework's established,
he carpets it, throws up drywall
                                        on opposite sides of his skin
& leaves it unfurnished,   places an ad in the paper
boasting of a 2-bedroom, 1 bath

in friendly surroundings   & a landlord easy to reach;
yet, for months, he goes unrented,

since symbolically he's the definition
of distant & difficult to fit into,   a faulty structure
lacking the soul most tenants seek.

 ADAM BYKO

FIVE THEORIES CONCERNING THE BIRDS AT THE TIP OF MY TONGUE

1. The birds replace a lie.

I felt the flutter in my throat before she even asked the question.

"Do you love me?"

It hung in the air over her spacious bed, the mattress almost as wide as her bedroom. I did everything I could to keep my mouth shut. I bit at the inner corners of my cheeks. I held my breath and counted to ten. But the bubbling swelled up from the bottom of my stomach, feathers tickled at my uvula, and the first beak pried open my poorly sealed lips. The fourteen sparrows poured out of my mouth in a mad rustle of wings. Needless to say, Andrea was not amused.

"...The worst part is, I'm not even surprised."

She leaned back into her pillow, staring at the birds swirling beneath the textured cream of her ceiling. Her face was flushed, burning as if in sympathy with the red curls of hair teasing at the top of her nightdress.

I gestured helplessly. I grabbed her shoulder with one hand and pointed at my heart with the other. I tried to make her see the more nuanced truth. But her eyes never strayed from the ceiling, even as the sparrows settled one by one at the foot of her bed. The sparrow with a white spot on his beak—the one my mother named Lionel—chirped his way up the mashed potato contours of Andrea's down comforter. He turned to face each of us, jerking his head from side to side with stop-motion suddenness.

A long, chest-rattling yawn unhinged my jaw, and Lionel hopped into my mouth. His thirteen companions followed, rushing down my throat. They always felt cold and fluid going back down, like little bustling icicles. I closed my mouth a little prematurely. A single tail feather snagged between my lips; I spat it out with as much delicacy as I could manage.

"Look," I said, massaging my jaw in recovery. "I know how this looks, but—"

"Oh save it, Adam." Andrea said, head still pressed back into the plush of her pillow. "I asked a question. You answered. What more is there to say?"

"Hold on. This isn't fair. You know I can't control it."

"I know, right? You can't help but be honest for once. It must be killing you."

I leaned over, trying to worm my way into her field of vision.

"You know it's more complicated than that. I... you've got to let me explain. Just because I can't answer right now, doesn't mean..."

"Actually, it's pretty simple," Andrea said quietly. She closed her eyes. "You say yes. Either you don't let things drag on for two years, or you say yes. Two options. Simple."

I slumped back onto my side of the bed. Upon closer examination, the texture on the ceiling looked like a network of veins. Not human, more like what appears in a leaf when it's held up to the sun—the thin film of its surface illuminated to show the labyrinth of machinery within.

Before lapsing into restless sleep, I imagined taking a razor to that puckered drywall. Slicing it clean and even, leaving the artistic embellishments of texture littered upon the bedroom floor. I scrubbed away the ambiguities and polished it down to its essential form. When I closed my eyes that night, I saw a ceiling simple and white.

Theory 2: The birds compensate for inadequacies of language.

The first time the sparrows made their appearance, my pajamas were soaked with urine. I had wet the bed, and stains of evidence trickled down to the rubber soles of my footie pajamas. I tried to shuffle to the bathroom without getting caught, being too old for this particular transgression at the age of six. My parents must have heard a floorboard creak because before I reached the bathroom door, my mother called to me from the hallway wearing a puffy white robe.

"Adam, is there something you want to tell me?"

Given our lack of experience with the bird phenomenon, our reactions to the forthcoming flutter of the fourteen sparrows were a little hysterical in retrospect. My mother screamed as the birds burst out of my mouth, zig-zagging as a swarm. At the time, I didn't know that the birds took my voice with them, so I tried to shout something about being sorry. I strained until I felt my neck pulse with the effort. Still, I couldn't produce a sound, leaving me crying voiceless little tears in frustration.

My father stumbled out of the room, eyes bleary and hair disheveled. He looked from the sparrows to my frantic mother to his urine-soaked son and back to the sparrows in cascading waves of astonishment. He wore only his sagging plaid boxers, clearly unprepared for any intervention. My mother begged for help as she swatted at the birds whizzing past. He still hadn't budged from the edge of the doorway when my jaw unhinged and the sparrows came rushing back down my throat to my simultaneous terror and relief.

As time went on, my mother adjusted to this peculiar trait. She set birdfeeders throughout the house. When she asked a question that prompted an avian onslaught, she waited patiently for the birds to take their course before rephrasing her line of inquiry. One of the sparrows even took to her presence, often resting on her shoulder. My mother named him Lionel, and she would offer extra handfuls of seeds to his white-spotted beak.

My father, however, never quite grew accustomed to the fourteen sparrows. He especially distrusted protestations regarding my lack of control over the bird-swarms. After I missed every college application deadline, my father cornered me in the kitchen, asking what I could possibly have been thinking. As soon as my jaw began to unhinge, my father's face changed. The crinkles around his eyes flattened, and an unholy hue of purple seeped into his face. He shook, and a strand of gray hair escaped from his spackled comb-over to dance across his forehead.

The birds rushed out in their cacophony of chirps and wing-rustles.

"NO!" my father roared, closing the space between us in pounding steps.

Lionel perched on top of the refrigerator and tilted his head sideways.

"You make this stop right now!" my father hissed. His breath felt hot. He grabbed me by the shoulders. I mouthed *I can't*, but this only made my father tighten his grip.

Lionel watched the scene unfold with beady-eyed impassivity. His thirteen sparrow brethren took advantage of some dishes soaking in the sink for an impromptu bird bath.

"Don't give me that.... Bullshit." My father never cursed and the word spat from his lips like it boiled out of his stomach. "I *know*. No one else can figure this nonsense out. The doctors, the psychiatrists, they're all stumped. But I know. You think this..." waving his arms at the sparrows now fluttering out of the sink, "will protect you. You think this gets you off the hook. I don't know how you do it, but I will. Not. Tolerate it. Not anymore. You have to answer for yourself, the same as anyone else."

Lionel flew down and perched upon my father's shoulder. My father swung his hand and clipped Lionel with a desperate slap.

"ENOUGH!"

Spittle dripped from my father's lips. The sparrows flew into the next room, leaving me mute in the kitchen. My father ranted on, screaming about not "putting up with the charade" and "restoring a sense of sanity." He had turned over to the counter, whispering to himself about "this unacceptable...elaborate evasion of responsibility and discourse," when my jaw finally dropped and the sparrows returned. My father didn't turn around, so he didn't see Lionel give him one long fluttering look before finally diving down my throat.

*   *   *

Needless to say, the dozen notecards I carried with me to the lectern never mentioned the fourteen sparrows. The previous speaker had been a coworker of my father's at the university, an exceptionally tall man with a telescoping neck. I tilted the microphone down, and it screeched in response to my touch. Sweat beaded on my forehead.

I looked out at the sea of dark suits and tasteful dresses. I felt my tie constrict around my windpipe. My notecards were out of order. I tried to find my first one, the one with the specific joke about my father being a Detroit Lions fan (something about death being sweet relief by comparison). My father's casket was open to my left. I caught a glimpse of the unreal wax of his face. I grabbed the lectern and tried to reconcile the flood of memories washing over me into a human being, something I could breathe back into the world even after it had been taken away.

Instead, I only found sparrows. They rushed out over the crowd, to a general spirit of agitation. I slapped the wooden lectern in frustration; the thump beneath the microphone was lost amidst the chaos. The flurry of wings settled faster than I thought possible. I looked up and squinted through a hot watery glaze. Someone had set a bird-feeder in the back of the room. I found my mother in the front row, stroking the underside of Lionel's chin.

Theory 3: The birds give form to a soul escaping a body.

I awoke to racing farmland. Dirt sprayed in all directions, chattering against the roof of the car with prying insistence.

The roof of the car. I was in a car.

The steering wheel looked like a snake eating its own tail in my hands.

In the rearview mirror, I caught a heat-stained glimmer of asphalt road receding into the background. Hand over hand, I turned the car with sweat-soaked panic. It skidded across the freshly plowed earth, wobbling in slalom zig-zags until the tires finally gained traction. I wanted to merge back onto the road at a diagonal, to settle back onto the correct course of travel with grace and ease. The summer haze made the approaching stretch of soil ripple in the glare. I squinted and pulled down the driver-side sunvisor.

I realized too late that the soil was not soil. The property ended with a pond. In the briefest of seconds, my front tires whirred through open air, caught between solid and liquid—true interstate travel. I felt a wrenching sense of abbreviation, like a record stopped midway through a song. I opened my mouth to cry out, to unleash my frustration and my terror and my indignation with righteous fury.

The car didn't provide much space for the fourteen sparrows. They rattled against the roof, pecked impotently at windows as they searched for an exit. All except Lionel, who settled upon the dashboard. We stared at each other, and I loosened my grip on the wheel. Water seeped through the door. I took a deep breath and looked out the window.

I had lodged myself in the shallows, the water only surged halfway up the car door. I lowered my driver-side window and let the fourteen sparrows flutter away into the sky. I watched them twirl gracefully in silhouette against the sun. Spiraling ever upward, drinking in the freedom of higher altitudes. Meanwhile, I sat inside my dripping metal cage. I wondered what would happen if my foot pressed down on the accelerator, whether Lionel and the rest could map out every inch of the sky between them if I was gone.

I climbed out the window and lay back on the scalding metal roof. The car shifted a little beneath my weight, but it wasn't going anywhere. I did my best to seal my lips. The sparrows would come back, I knew. Their freedom was not mine to grant. The rules didn't work that way.

Still, I didn't see the need to rush. I'd relax before wading to shore, before approaching the bewildered farmer with a sheepish request for help. I'd let the heat of the moment soak in through my back and only leave when it saturated my every pore. For the second time that day, I let myself rest.

Theory 4: The birds offer(ed) a finite representation of a vivid emotional experience (one which necessarily dulls over time).

The fireflies arrived like morning frost, conjured from the shadows with imperceptible grace. Last week, Hazel asked me what they did during the day. Did the bugs fly all around us with their inner light muted or did they hide until their appointed hour? I honestly didn't know. Her little face was scrunched up in anticipation, ready for her world to make a little bit more sense, to become a little bit more rational. The world feels so big when you're five, so overwhelming. Your days are too full of possibility. You need to make sense of the vast network of life that surrounds you, to shrink down its mysteries to a more manageable size. You want to learn how to see the world as an ordinary, unremarkable thing.

After thinking about her question for a good minute, I did the only thing I could. I lied.

I told Hazel that the fireflies were visitors from another planet. During the day, they lived comfortably on their home world, playing little insect games and going to their little insect jobs. But at night, they travelled. They grabbed hold of a beam of light from the nearest star and raced across the universe. They landed on our planet still full of starlight, blinking with galactic residue. If you catch a firefly and hold it close, you can feel the fabric of the universe in your hand. It tickles.

I rubbed my eyes, and the rich smell of gasoline radiated from my hands. Hazel ran across the fresh-cut lawn, blinking lights flitting away from her outstretched fingers. Danielle hip-checked the screen door open, two glasses of chilled Franzia in hand.

"She catch any yet?"

I shook my head, taking one glass away by the stem. Wine sloshed out and a sweet, red stain blossomed upon the hardwood porch. I wet my thumb and tried to smudge away the worst of the damage. Danielle leaned back in the wicker lawn chair, and its creaking spine harmonized with the chirping katydids.

"Probably for the best. Don't need any questions about why these aliens look exactly like ordinary bugs."

Danielle eyed me playfully over her glass as she took a drink. She didn't quite approve of how I addressed the big questions for Hazel, but she didn't have the heart to fight for anything different.

"Please. What bug could possibly glow in the dark? Ya gotta admit, I'm providing a way more rational explanation."

Danielle sighed and stretched her legs out so that her toes curled over the porch ledge. She'd taken off her shoes and loosened her hair but otherwise still wore her office clothes. After landing the management job, her days had started getting longer. It eroded at her, and she came home less intact each day. I could see the weariness etch itself around her eyes. I had my hands full with Hazel, but I sympathized. It had been some time since I last felt myself being whittled away.

*   *   *

It used to be different. Back when Hazel was only taking her first leg-shiveringly uncertain steps, I still worked at the firm. Not in a position of authority or anything, nothing impressive like Danielle has now, but still, it was a grind. I took to jogging in the mornings. I'd stretch out at the edge of dawn and pound my frustration into the pavement during those early violet hours. We lived on the outskirts of a suburban town, a little single-story ranch house off a winding back-road. Most mornings, I wouldn't see a soul.

I had a secret. I didn't run for the exercise, not for the bliss of pain or the burning peace of a runner's high. Instead, I ran so I could scream.

After getting a mile or so away from the house, I would stop on the shoulder of the road. I would lean forward, hands on my knees, sweat stinging my eyes. I would think about my coming workday, about the mounting piles of files, and the encroaching deadlines. I would hear the avalanche of days dedicated to the firm, the slow rumble of lost time. I would feel the hollow in my chest where the job had gnawed away, the corrosive rot of life ill-spent. My future evaporating into mist.

At this point, I would pull every last sense of decay and frustration from the pit of my stomach. I would look up to the sky and prepare a primal yell. And, invariably, the fourteen sparrows would race out.

I don't know if this ritual was healthy, but it brought me some modicum of comfort. I kept it up for months on end, never failing even in the driving rain. On one such morning, I released the sparrows into the air. A car approached from around the bend. Its headlights stretched long white fingers through the raindrops. I let the sparrows fly a little longer than usual rather than risk distracting the driver. Once the car disappeared over the hill-crest, I yawned my mouth wide. Fifteen birds began to dive.

Lionel reached home first, and I almost gagged. He had bulleted down at an unnatural speed, faster than ever before. The others followed, and as I counted, I realized that there was one bird too many. A massive grey hawk swooped in pursuit, wings outstretched. I waved my arms helplessly, imploring the sparrows to dive faster. They thunked into my stomach in pairs, seven-eight, nine-ten, eleven-twelve. The thirteenth sparrow barely reached my mouth when I saw a puff of feathers and blood soaked talons. The hawk swooped up, barely flapping its charcoal wings to return to higher altitudes. The carcass of the fourteenth sparrow dangled, dripping red through the rain.

From that point forward, I found myself accompanied by at least one placid, grey hawk on every run. They followed me in wide, arcing ovals, leaving my field of vision only to return in greater numbers. I kept my mouth closed and swallowed my screams, but still the hawks persisted. By the end of the week, I found four of them roosting on the top of our ranch house, flapping slowly into motion as I broke into a jog.

I don't know how I thought it would end. I suppose I thought I could outlast them. I could show them that I had nothing to offer, and, after a time, they would have to accept that reality and move along. So I kept my routine in spite of their relentless pursuit. Each morning, I slipped away from Danielle and tiptoed past Hazel's room. I faced the hawks and accepted their challenge.

The trouble was, I had grown accustomed to the daily release. Without an avenue for my screams, my frustrations simmered. A nagging pain throbbed at my temple, and I found myself snapping at colleagues at work. Worse, I found my patience winnowing down with Hazel. She would throw her plastic spork to the ground with a gleeful laugh, and I'd pound the table, saying "Fine, eat like an animal then" as I walked away. I took long trips to the bathroom, sitting on the toilet with my head between my hands in search of some form of center.

So, when I finally tripped over a fallen branch a quarter mile away from the house, I couldn't help crying out in frustration. My mouth swung open. The hawks began to dive.

In wild-eyed desperation, I tried to cover my mouth with my hands. Of course that was never an option. The rules did not allow it. The sparrows broke past my locked fingers and scattered in thirteen different directions. They tried to dart away, but the hawks were too determined. In graceful swoops, the hawks plucked my sparrows from the air one by one. I waved my arms and spat wordless curses. I tried to stretch my mouth open as far as it would go. But my jaw would come not come undone. Four sparrow corpses were carried away. The other nine had disappeared into the trees behind me, chirping in abject panic.

I kept prying at my jaw, trying to force an end to the process. In the distance, metallic grey wings pierced the sky. The hawks were coming back.

"Come on, come on, come on," I mouthed to myself, now slapping my face in the hopes of jarring something loose. Finally, unrelated to my efforts, my jaw dropped. The sparrows emerged from the woods to return home. With wings pinned back, the hawks carved the space between us.

One-two-three, down the back of my throat. I tapped at my thigh impatiently. Four-five-six. As the final three sparrows made their attempt to flutter home, I found Lionel bringing up the rear. The white spot on his beak glinted in the faintest stream of morning light. A hawk reached for him with claws outstretched. With the loudest voiceless cry I could muster, I leapt and swatted at the massive bird. It gouged away at my palm, tearing a jagged scar across the skin. I dropped to my knees and pressed my injured hand to my stomach. On the berm of the road, two feet away, Lionel lay prone in a tiny pool of sparrow blood.

I dove over and scooped him with my good hand. I pressed him to my chest, and the hawks retreated to a higher plane. I looked down and found a puncture in his right wing. His inkwell eyes darted in distress.

I carried him back home and woke Danielle. Without me saying a word, she knew what to do. She tended to Lionel's wing with a makeshift band-aid tourniquet while I wrapped my injured hand to the best of my ability. After double-wrapping the improvised bandage with scotch tape, she brought Lionel up to my mouth. He was cold and fluid all the way down, like a little bustling icicle.

Afterward, when I told her what happened, Danielle was furious. She gritted her teeth and left for a shower. When she got out, she told me that she was going back to work again. I didn't get a say.

"We pick each other up," she said, over the sound of her hair dryer. "But that only works if you tell me when you're falling."

*   *   *

Out on the porch, we watched Hazel chase a particularly evasive firefly. It drifted right in front of her face only to float just out of reach once it caught her attention.

"Come back!" she shouted. "I wanna feel the universe!"

The firefly danced up over the porch railing. It hovered by my wine glass before landing upon a hook-shaped scar on my right hand. Its feet felt like eyelashes. Danielle watched with a tired smile.

"So, how does it feel? The fabric of the universe, I mean?"

Nine sparrows stirred in my stomach before she even asked the question.

Theory 5: The birds are the inner nameless, discrete from (and vulnerable to) the outer nameless.

My mother requested a hospice with bird-feeders.

This proved more difficult to find than might be expected. It's not exactly a feature that gets listed in promotional brochures, so I had to call each facility and ask about their status, vis-a-vis bird-feeder availability. Some were quick no's, while others promised to call back after looking into the issue (and rarely did). Finally, I found one that answered yes quickly and without equivocation. It was farther away than most of the other options and more expensive, providing small cabins for residents rather than simple rooms. Still, my mother was insistent.

"I don't want to push you, Adam, but honestly, it's not like I'm going to be calling in a whole lot of favors after this. Let's just make sure we do this with everyone as comfortable as possible."

In her typical fashion, I don't think Mom was talking about herself.

Each visit required a two-hour drive up a mountainside. Danielle called off as often as she could, but life's banal demands kept dragging her back. So most days, I drove with the passenger seat empty—Hazel drooling little puddles of sleep into her scarf in the back.

At home, spring melted its way across the lawn. Swollen crocus buds wriggled their way to the surface, vibrant purple seams prying at the edges of unfolding. Up at Mom's place, though, winter lingered. Grass crunched beneath your shoes and icy clouds puffed with every breath. The transition was jarring, like falling into a snow globe and finding a world cocooned in stasis.

Radio signals fuzzed out during the climb, so I used my phone to cue up some Chopin nocturnes. The piano trickled out of my car speakers with liquid delicacy. It always sent Hazel spiraling past the rim of consciousness, but I needed something to soften the edge of my nerves. Fog collected along the cliffside bends. I could see it coming like some glaucoma smudging at the corner of my eye, but there was never any avoiding it. Instead, I just had to slow down and knife my way through the uncertainty. It required concentration, finding a path through the murk, a level of mental effort that sent my teeth into grinding motion. Chopin didn't totally alleviate the strain, but it helped buoy my patience. In the face of temporary conditions, I don't need relief so much as a reminder that they cannot last.

Sure enough, eventually the fog retreated. I turned along the precipices with more confidence, accelerating to make up for lost time. We reached the long gravel drive that led to the complex right around noon; Hazel awoke to the popcorn patter of rocks leaping beneath our tires. To the best of her knowledge, Grandma was at camp. We checked in at the visitor's center—a pale, circular brick structure at the end of the drive. The secretary offered us wristbands and provided Hazel with a small scavenger hunt, full of plants and rocks found in the woods behind the residences.

We followed a packed dirt trail past the numbered wooden cabins. The tumor hadn't affected Mom's mobility much, so she had been granted a cabin toward the rear end of the premises. I let Hazel run ahead, eager to complete her perfunctory visit so she could start her scavenger hunt. The grounds were too small for her to get far. After a few long strides, I was back beside her, waiting at the door to cabin 14.

I set tea boiling on the stove while my mother sat at her kitchen table, watching Hazel through the frosted window. Hazel's red scarf streamed behind her as she raced along the wooded outskirts. Its tassels danced like candle-flames on flickering wicks.

"You did good with that one," Mom said, still fixed upon the scene playing outside her window. She absently curled a thin wisp of grey hair around her finger. "As far as granddaughters go, I think you really went above and beyond.... It's the one on the far left, dear."

I had been opening cupboard after cupboard looking for the cups. Foreign territory complicated the simplest of tasks. After pouring the boiling water into a pair of nondescript pale blue mugs, I joined my mother at the table. I pressed my palms against the cup and let warmth seep through the ceramic.

"Yeah, I don't get credit for her, though. Honestly, no idea how we've gotten this far without scarring her for life."

"Oh, I'm sure you already have," Mom waved her hand dismissively. "That's what parents are for. We mess everything up and hope that you turn out just functional enough to put the pieces back together."

"Real comforting, mom. Really reassuring stuff."

"See, I'm doing it again! I've got one foot out the door, and I'm still doing damage."

"Don't say that," I said, quietly. "The one foot out the door part, I mean. The parts about how you're causing irrevocable psychological harm, those parts are all fine. Let's just keep both of your feet here though."

My mother took a sip of her tea. Steam misted her narrow oval glasses. She took them off and wiped at the clouds with the bottom of her shirt.

"Now, Adam, you don't really get a say in that."

"Well, I'm gonna try anyway. That's what I do."

She put the glasses back on and a small wistful smile tugged at her lips.

"You know, there's someone I've been waiting to see. Before I go."

"I promise you, Danielle is coming out next visit. She's just a little swamped right now but —"

"I think you know I'm not talking about Danielle. ... you've given me so many unexpected visits over the years, but this time, I'm making it a request. I need to see Lionel, Adam."

I set my tea down on the table, my face flushed. The long trip, my daughter—her only granddaughter—right outside the expensive cabin, somehow this wasn't enough. No, she had to ask for something I couldn't give.

"Christ, you're just as bad as Dad. You know that's not how this works—"

"Oh hush now," Mom said. She placed her elbow on the table and rested her chin on her hand. Her soft green eyes peered out from behind the glasses. "I just have one more question for you. What's going to happen to me when I die?"

Her face broke into a wide grin. I struggled to bite down on my tongue to avoid giving her the satisfaction.

"Now don't be difficult." she said. "You tell me what happens to me, to all my experiences, my dreams, my innermost consciousness after I die... Well?"

The nine sparrows charged out despite my best efforts. Eight settled by the baseboard heater, basking in its unnatural warmth. Lionel never flew quite as well after the incident with the hawks, but he still hopped along the table until he reached my mother's cup. With some effort, he perched himself upon the rim. My mother lifted the mug slow and steady to her lips and whispered some inaudible secret to the sparrow. She set the cup back down and let Lionel nibble seeds out of her hand.

I looked out the frosted window. I could barely catch a glimpse of Hazel's red scarf through the trees. I thought of hawks and wolves and vicious wild things. Lionel crunched a seed, his wounded wing curled by his side. My mother's face was aglow, radiating bliss with each peck at the center of her palm.

The red scarf disappeared entirely. I listened to the scattered pieces of my voice chirping through the cabin. Steam unspooled from my tea in liquid threads. I took one long, burning drink and waited for the moment when everything comes back.

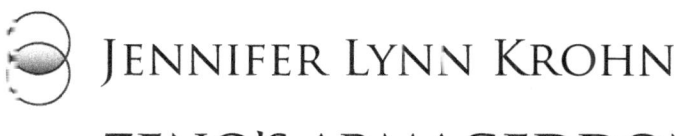

JENNIFER LYNN KROHN

ZENO'S ARMAGEDDON

A purple streak slits open
the sky. *The comet,*
father says *is halfway here.*

The next night, white moths—
a snow storm on our back porch.
Father says *It's halfway here.*

At dawn, I venture down streets,
where concrete glitters with galaxies
of broken glass. I return with a bag

full of canned artichoke hearts
and beets—all I could find.
Father says *It's halfway here.*

At sunset, we start a fire. A dozen
other fires dot the hillside.
Regardless of the wood we feed it,

we cannot warm the starry night.
Father says *It's halfway here.*
God has answered my prayers

for the first time in my life.
That first week, I whispered *Please!*
Please, don't let it arrive,

but faced with constant suspense
I repent my request. Hospitals empty.
Ambulances abandoned. Why save

a life if death is tomorrow
or the next day or the day after that?
No one sees that the comet

has changed nothing. Death stands
in the same place he always had.
We wake to a herd of deer in search

of water. My father squints up
and says *It's halfway here*. Exhausted,
I mutter *Let's just get this over with*.

 JUNED SUBHAN

THREE POEMS

THE FATHER

We stopped by the edge of the pavement,
motionless, looking –
on the road: a wreathe of roses, weak and pink
as leukaemia in summer – and

my husband's cold hand
curled into mine, tight as a ticking, gold clock.

"This is where our child died," he whispered,
his words as thin as his powder-blue shirt,

and I saw –

a sleek, black limousine
passing silently down the road, the reflection
of a child's coffin against its shiny glass,
rose petals falling behind it,
and passing us again but slower this time with its windows

blacked out.

We glanced across the street,
at our neighbour's large front yard –

noticing

a bustle of fathers in green T-shirts lugging buckets of hot coal
and barbecues with mothers and children,
fathers painting the mothers'
and children's faces with licks of blinding light –

while beyond their gaiety, in summer's festive glare,
I saw an apiary of angry bees in a different garden behind
our neighbour's home, twisting into
a dark cloud in the sky,

and I thought –

we used to revel with them
once – and whatever joy the fathers
share with their families, that could all disappear

in a

split second.

My husband's grip loosened,
just as the fathers opened their mouths
and shielded their gaze –

a child's scream, and
the blossom of screaming glass and metal
blooming in splinters in the air,
like shattered teeth.

The bees rose higher in the sky –
a thick, black veil
weeping over a funeral –

and the fathers across from us
turned their heads,
as though not viewing us as one of them
but strangers on this side of the street,

their eyes shutting then opening
in bright, empty glances.

For a split second, I believed I saw my
husband there,
with the other fathers, a father himself,

painting our child's face
and my face with light.

THE MOTHER

"This is where our child's balloons floated,"
my husband reminded me,

holding

onto a balloon himself as he withdrew
into the chasm of his own shadow,

a shadow

floating from one empty room
into another in our spacious home,
then shrinking
into the silhouette of a small child
against a wall in the long hallway.

Meanwhile,

I glanced across the back garden –

those red wellington boots and
a child's spade beside
the sandcastle and the empty, silver swing
in the warm breeze and a strip of dead, yellow flowers –

at another mother's back garden with its
ghostly tree ferns and the tall scarecrow erected in the middle,
suited-up in a pair of grey trousers,
a double-breasted jacket,
cream shirt, burgundy bow-tie,
and a black trilby hat like a father – and the mother

hanging

her children's dazzling summer clothes and
pretty birthday dresses
on the washing line.

She slipped inside her
bright, humid conservatory in which she kept
a flock of buzzards, and
as soon as she slipped inside,

the birds flapped and cried hysterically,

in the air,

and around her,

until I feared she might be swallowed
whole by those birds, except
as a mother she opened her arms and laughed,

her laughter imbued with heartache
and joy,

in a way only a mother's can be
as if she'd lived and breathed
and only knew real heartache.

The buzzards finally settled, and
as the mother swept up the fallen feathers with a stiff broom,
she glanced across at me
then looked away.

That night, while I slept
I dreamt the scarecrow shivered into life –
a father shifting into the gloom of my child's room,
then grasping onto the string of one of his
grey balloons, floating up in the air too –

as the mother next door,
in the same dream approached me in
church on Sunday, scarfed lavender in her own sorrow,
saying to me –

Here, take one of these, it will help you grieve
like I grieve –

handing to me in my embrace
one of her birds in a crib blanket,
still sound asleep it seemed,
such a small, little thing –

just like a mother's joy,
and just like heartache.

THE CHILD

"Look out –" my husband said in the car as I
drove along the road, away from our neighbourhood –

and looking out I saw a tall scarecrow hanging suspended
in the starched-blue sky, unmoving, its hands tied to a cluster of balloons.

I continued driving while my husband glanced in the mirror,
catching the sun, and the silhouette of our child still playing on the street,

as an empty car glided slowly past us – a glimmer of bees
smashed against its rear window and a wreathe of falling roses.

I saw for the final time a mother in her front room teeming with children,
each one like a stiff mannequin, and she danced around them,

during this summer and all other summers to come. I
noticed her face filled with heartache as she kissed each one

of her children, wondering why they didn't blink – and
next to her house, an elderly man buried a black suit and a dress.

"Where are we going?" my husband suddenly asked, *"where? –"*
as another empty car glided past us in silence –

the open road stretching before us, touching the white horizon, and
in the distance across a yellow field, the scarecrow finally came crashing down,

laughing and screaming its head off – in a squall of birds,
and wings, and the moment he exploded –

above us, the sun turned into the colour of heartache too.
Then, when I peered back, no longer looking ahead –

a shower of broken glass – I saw for a moment, our child
sat in the backseat, stroking a bird on his lap, alive,

and I reached out to touch him, feeling him once more
for a brief second, a flash, and then – *"where?"*

 JOAN EYLES JOHNSON

ONE CANNIBAL WAITING

Picture this: A tiny island wild and beautiful of course because no person has ever stepped foot on it before it is one of many such islands all clustered together somewhere far from the known world pristine and clear of disorder So I go there one day maybe by accident a shipwreck or mutiny or for whatever strange reason weird things happen of course I find myself wading through the azure water and dipping my toes in sugary sand and think perhaps I've found paradise on earth at last I intend to live out my days eating coconuts and lobsters and communing with palm trees which I shall name and no madman is going to find me and no bad news is going to zap me and I will never pay any income taxes ever again of course and then *picture this*: one day after many blissful days of contemplation of my suntanned body and beautiful muscles I hear something behind me and I turn to see crashing through the bushes a person a man at least it looks like a man or at least it once was a man or will be one day a man it is surely some relative of the apes it approaches me of course with its arms raised high in anger or supplication I don't know and I realize that this is one of those islands straight out of Melville and god how I miss my books but here is reality pumping adrenaline through me like an orgasm and this creature is going to do me some harm in fact this is the last cannibal on earth and I am his breakfast lunch or dinner depending on his concept of time I scream of course my voice surprises me after all these days unused I have always had a kind of cynicism some shoe was going to drop and earthquakes follow me wherever I move and there is always a letter in the mailbox sooner or later impending doom irony typical and now this: one last cannibal.

JENNIFER MACBAIN-STEPHENS

THE TELEPHONE OPERATOR KNOWS WHEN TO PLUG IN

the operator whispers "quixotic"
illegally enters the conversation

mouths "cabin crew"
and "patient zero" She (I) am made deaf

I haven't seen the sun for days
but I heard it once

a mixture of arrows and static
every word a broken economy

the operator resonates in outer space
presses all of the wrong

buttons and expects a different outcome
each time

it's not the line I was looking for
but the blood in my veins turns stagnant

a bread line moves faster
which pleases the operator

since returning to Russia
in the past, sits behind a scratchy curtain

eyebrows like daggers
a speech class weapon

eyes and lips
call me a Slavic slur

the snow on the line falls
over icy insults

the scrabble dictionary sluggish
give me your dirt

the operator whispers
plays the soundtrack to the

The Third Man
listens in, but this isn't Orson Welles

in black and white beauty
it's our own Vienna getaway

and the operator is taking notes
tired of the spoken word

the codes change too fast:

"A red dress flies at_____"
"opulence colors my_____"

cut throat with a snap
I hear the busy signal

my voice falters
free fall streaming and radio world

all of the dimes fall from behind my ears
try to crawl toward my eyes

I'm a reborn manikin
the operator breaks the fourth wall

dresses me for the opera
I wear a dial up receiver hat and electrical

tape purse, a bodice covered in numbers
the operator always wanted to say "you look like

a million," injects a syringe into my arm,
retires to a box seat

TIM SUERMONDT

A DRAGON FLYING THROUGH AN OPEN WINDOW

Of course it doesn't. Of course it does.
What a world where everything is possible
and impossible.

A man who's on the cusp of living forever
dies alone.
A woman plants seeds in her backyard garden

and skyscrapers grow like voracious fireflies
and a manuscript
is retrieved from the desert of the unknowns.

I hop on the dragon and we fly through that
window together
into the hot afternoon air, birds stopping

in midflight to watch us loop and ascend out
of sight,
no more knowing where we're going than I do.

CHARLES WILKINSON

THE CHEERFUL GOWN

All night someone had been trying to teach Latin to Mr Lark. When he awoke early, with the same sense of confusion he'd experienced at failing to grasp the ablative absolute at the age of nine, neither the voice nor the place reminded him of anything in his past. He was left with a fading image of sunlight on bare white walls, floorboards silver with dust. The speaker was invisible, no more than the persistence of declensions repeated in a firm voice, although with pauses to enlarge on elusive grammatical points. He had never been much of a classicist. Why, he asked himself, now he'd reached pensionable age, was he dreaming in a dead language? Perhaps the little that had been drilled into him was being saved—or erased?

As soon as he'd shaved and dressed, he went down to the kitchen. Aunt was already in the small sitting room, which overlooked the garden. Through the open door, he could see her brown hand, gnarled with arthritis, at peace on the armrest, the television above the cabinet and the window with its views of jackdaws, their silver streaked heads shining in the morning sunlight as they plundered the bird table.

'Is that you, Leonard?' Aunt's frail voice was strong enough to rise above the babble of expertise on *Everyday Antiques*.

Who else could it possibly be? Then he remembered the plumbers. He edged closer to the door. 'Just me, Aunt. The men are coming later.'

On the T.V. the presenter, wearing a blue hat with a preposterously broad brim and a red cravat that clashed with his canary yellow linen jacket, wandered around an outdoor market. He was accompanied by an elderly couple dressed in violet shell suits bearing the *Everyday Antiques* logo.

'He's just made them buy a decanter almost exactly like the one I gave your uncle. We had it all our married lives.'

Mr Lark recalled the decanters on the sideboard in the gloomy house where Aunt had lived until the death of her husband. Her furniture, along with the more valuable paintings, porcelain and glassware, was in the shed. Nothing would be sold until it was time for her to go into a home.

'I'm going to the mini-mart,' he called out.

'Well, I wouldn't pay that. Not for a clock that's broken.'

'I won't be long.'

As he went through the dining-room, he saw someone had draped a red dressing-gown over the chair at the head of the table. He picked the garment up, holding it out at arm's length. The material was extraordinarily soft and would be gentle on bare skin. It was far too large for Aunt; it would reach well below his knees. The collar and cuffs were quilted. Perhaps it was a smoking jacket. Although it looked new, there was no label. He rearranged it neatly on the chair and went out to the front hall.

A sparkling day in late October and the last of the autumn colours clinging to the trees. If he turned left and went up into the High Street, he was practically certain to meet someone he knew. In his experience people were best avoided unless it was necessary to conduct essential business. He decided to take the country route along by the ruined castle and then visit the supermarket on the further edge of the small town. Once he was past the bungalows, he was on a narrow lane flanked by high hedgerows. He heard animals moving; the almost human cough of a cow. There were no cottages. He'd been walking for about five minutes when he heard someone singing a hymn on the other side of the hedge: a man's voice, a baritone, more or less in tune. As Mr Lark drew level with the gate, a stick arced across a field to be followed by a black and white sheepdog accelerating from a slink. Before its master could come into view, Mr Lark quickened his pace, his eyes firmly on the way ahead.

When he turned the corner, he saw the beech, ash and oak on the slopes below the castle mound had kept their foliage, reds, copper, a rich orange and russet warm with the last radiance of summer life. As he approached, the depth of colour seemed to come, not with the cold eastern light, which clarified the landscape of fields and streams lined with feathery trees opening on his left, but from an unfading store of fire beyond. For a moment, he felt that if he went on further he would find himself subsumed into the autumn of an adjacent world.

When he returned home, he heard a hammering and the clank of metal from the floor above. The plumbers must have arrived while he was out. For weeks now they had been chasing the leaks and floods around the house. They had no sooner fixed the dripping from the pipes in the bathroom, which had affected the living room below, than a radiator on the landing malfunctioned. The problems with the storage tank in the attic ensured that the outflow gushed like a Roman fountain.

He put down the carrier bags in the kitchen and turned towards the sitting-room.

His aunt's hand was no longer on the armrest; instead, he could see the tip of one of her sensible brown shoes just below an expanse of stocking.

'I'm back!' he shouted.

'It's outrageous,' she said. 'I'm going to get Leonard to do something about it. '

On *Everyday Antiques* the presenter was now wearing a lilac jacket. He was indoors talking to an auctioneer whose long pale face was ossified with disdain. In front of them was a carved wooden chest with a pattern of leaves and acorns around the edge. Mr Lark was sure he'd seen something very similar before.

'Don't worry about the noise, Aunt. It's the men working.'

'Just wait until I speak to him.'

When Mr Lark went back through the dining-room, he noticed the red gown on the chair had vanished. Was it the day when the cleaner was due? Her aptitude for moving clothing and laundry around the house at whim was unrivalled. After lunch he discovered the dressing-gown hanging on the hall peg closest to the staircase.

~

Of course they'd all decided she was stupid when in fact Aunt was very far from it. Hadn't she realised that the antique dealers who'd visited her when she was in her own home were ghosts? The one with the long gray hair, yellowing above the ears, curling over his collar, was long dead. At that time Leonard had taken to coming over two or three times a week to talk about 'downsizing' and a getting good price for the furniture that wouldn't fit into a flat. He'd been most upset when she'd turned down a good offer for the grandfather clock. 'I'll not see that old ghost's money this side of the grave and, once I'm "promoted to glory," as they say in the Sally Army, I won't have any use for it.' Leonard had insisted that the old man, Mr Silverstein, was alive and running a highly profitable concern in the High Street. Aunt had merely looked her nephew in the eye and announced 'I was in a world war. I know a dead man when I see one.'

~

The next morning Mr Lark was later than usual in setting off for the mini-mart. As it was Monday, which in the town had long had the status of a second Sunday, he decided to risk the short cut through the High Street. The sharp frost had freshened the air, leaving a white line of ice under the eaves on the darker side of the road. There was a light on the hairdressing salon; its windows were streaked with condensation. None of the cafés had opened. At the far end of the street, two men were manoeuvring a wardrobe into a shop that sold furniture, curios and complete runs of dusty old magazines.

It was quiet in the mini-mart. Since the rebranding there were fewer customers and never anyone to serve them. The regulars, who'd gossiped with the owners when it had been a corner shop, disliked the self-service machines. A young couple, clearly hikers passing through, examined the soft drinks cabinet, then took out a bottle of mineral water, which they returned before leaving. Now the place was empty; even the piped music was barely audible. Without the pressure of a crowd, Mr Lark was at leisure to compare prices and consider products he had never seen fit to purchase before. There was little to do at home, although he would've liked to solve the riddle of the red dressing-gown, which had somehow removed itself from the hall and was now on the battered sofa on the first floor landing. When questioned, Aunt had diverted her attention from *Everyday Antiques* for just long enough to deny all previous knowledge of the garment and its progress about the house.

Mr Lark scanned his few acquisitions, relieved as ever to have escaped the bored insolence of eyes at the check-out. He glanced at his watch. The cafés that opened on Mondays would have done so by now. He would return the long way round.

As he turned onto the back lane, he noticed the trees below the grey ruined castle had shed their leaves. The light shone evenly in the windless winter morning; the exposed boughs stripped to patterns of unbearable exactitude; not a solitary leaf softened the slender branches, frost-polished to a vitrified gleam, as if the smallest twig could cut. It was hardly credible that these structures had supported a superabundance of leaves, pale yellow, bronze, red and gold. The drifts of colours' spent wealth lay below, darkening from sepia to brown. Drawing level with the gate, he saw the dog with a stick in its mouth, as if its return had been suspended until he walked past again. Then the snuffling of cows at their winter feed, the same hymn being sung with a border lilt.

He stepped back into the faint warmth of home. There was no sound of the builders. Only the churning swoosh of the washing machine counterpointed by the tumble-drier's rhythmic clicks and scraping turns. The door leading to the utility room was ajar.

'Mrs N,' he called down, 'I'm back. Has my aunt had her tea?'

'I gives her that. And her ginger biscuit too. The both, she had.'

'Thank you. I'll leave your money on the hall table.'

'Funny, she was this morning. Thinks they're selling all her old bits and pieces on the box. Nonsense is what I tells her. There's more than one person as had a pearl necklace like that.'

'I'm sorry. She is a little confused at times. '

Then as he was about to go he remembered: 'Mrs N, I don't suppose you know anything about a red dressing-gown.'

'Well, I've seen it. Picked it up off the top staircase. I've put it over the banisters, haven't You'll not miss it.'

He decided against asking her how it came to be in the house at all. The lamp in the sitting-room cast a yellowish cone that stained the corner of the room by the bookcase, as if light itself were foxed. Aunt's left hand on the armrest again, the protruding veins tinged blue.

'Are you all right, Aunt?'

'Is that Leonard?'

'Yes, of course.'

'Good. There's something I want you to do. Phone the television people and tell them to stop selling my property. At once.'

It would be easier to go along with this. 'Yes, I'll do it now.'

He went out to the shed. No signs of the lock having being forced. Yet when he stepped inside he knew at once that the space was emptier. An uncluttered area of floor in front of him that he could not recall from his previous visit. The crates in the far corner were still there, alongside the dust sheets covering his aunt's furniture, powdered with the wings of dead moths. A grey light seeped in from a window. He drew back the closest sheet: a what-not, an eighteenth-century piece, on which she'd displayed her most precious porcelain. No doubt he'd stacked her possessions more neatly than he'd remembered: the simple explanation. And how could anything have been taken when there'd been no break-in?

~

After her fall, Aunt had been advised not to live alone. She recalled how plans for a flat were abandoned and she'd moved in with Leonard. Her misgivings about sharing accommodation with her nephew were soon dispelled and, after all, it had been her childhood home. The house was more than spacious enough for the two of them, and it was quiet, apart from the solitary television that was her companion. Leonard had long been too sensible to the emotions stirred by music to permit it to be played. There was so much to be said for silence, they agreed, although this was not a thought they would ever have expressed out loud. Some weeks she spoke to him less frequently than when he'd come to her home. Then his status as a visitor had required her to make conversation. Now they were under the same roof both of them understood the importance of not speaking without having a clear reason for disturbing the quietude, which was complete, but for the faint drip of the a leaking tap, the fact of enduring dust.

In poor condition, the house was a large place riddled by tiny rooms; it had a strange additional staircase that connected the attic to the ground floor, long corridors and landings laden with wooden chests and dysfunctional clocks, which had either wound down or displayed irregular hours. After the first few months, she colonised a couple of downstairs rooms, one with a good view of the garden.

Today she'd seen little of Leonard, although she was half aware of creaking in the room above her. She heard his soft footsteps outside followed by the door opening, first an inch or two and then wider; the faint clang and rattle of a tray and cutlery being put down on a table. She heard his voice claiming to have phoned the television people. They were looking into her complaint, he said.

Once he'd gone she went over to the television and turned up the volume. The programme was being broadcast from a town she'd never heard of. A bald mouse of man in a three-piece suit and a bow tie was talking to a hideous woman with blue rinsed hair whilst he turned a Crown Derby tureen upside down. Aunt was quite certain it had never belonged to her. Perhaps they'd finally had the decency to stop selling her belongings in public. As she watched a second man appeared. He was tall and unusually gaunt and wore a russet-coloured suit. Was he the part-owner of the tureen? In fact he appeared to have no connection to either the woman or the expert, both of whom were not so much studiously ignoring him as unaware of his existence. As they began to inspect a jug, the newcomer, who was in the foreground but only just in shot, began to unwrap a brown paper parcel. He then picked up what Aunt at first thought was a red blanket, but when he shook it out it was evidently a red dressing-gown, which he held quite still until she was sure that it was not fully a constituent part of the programme, but a mystery that had escaped from her own life or perhaps an emblem in another world.

~

When Leonard awoke it was after six thirty in the morning. In his sleep, he'd sensed unrest in the house. A noise coming from below. Had it been a part of his dream? He put his sweater on over his pyjamas and went downstairs. In the kitchen, a tap dripped, its persistence a memorial to past leaks, burst pipes and overflows; perhaps a forerunner of floods to come. A sliver of waxy yellow light beneath the sitting-room door and men's voices, familiar in tone and yet rhythmically strange. He half opened the door. *Everyday Antiques* was still on. The presenter was wearing a striped blazer of a kind favoured by rowing clubs and a panama hat. His Zapata moustache had flourished cruelly since previous programmes. He held out a silver cigarette box to a man in a pin-striped suit and lilac bow tie. They were speaking in Latin. As they passed the item between them and examined the hallmark, Mr Lark was surprised by a sudden fury. The cigarette box was clearly his late uncle's, presented to the old man on his retirement by the firm where he'd been employed for fifty years. Although he couldn't understand what the experts were saying, there was an exaggeratedly public school disdain in their manner, as if they were downplaying its provenance and value. Then he recalled he'd come down to investigate the disturbance. A sound surely too loud to be connected to events in the sitting room. Perhaps the force moving the red dressing-gown had now decided to turn over tables or send books clattering off shelves. He checked the ground floor rooms. Everything was in its rightful place. He put a finger on the rim of a vase on the mantelpiece; not the faintest vibration.

As he went back through the kitchen, he realised he'd not seen his aunt's hand on the armrest. Had she tried to get up and fallen towards the chaise longue, where she'd sometimes slept before becoming reluctant to leave the chair? The rap of the gavel, almost simultaneous with a monosyllabic snap: *sold!* He pushed the door open as far as it would go: Aunt's sensible shoes in the middle of the carpet, one on its side, as though it had been kicked off; no one in the armchair or on the chaise longue.

'Aunt?'

Nothing. Apart from *Everyday Antiques* and the camera moving from presenter to auctioneer. *And the next lot is a wedding ring; three diamonds set in a band of gold.* At least they were speaking in English. *What am I bid?* And then a close up: the ring on its bed of black velvet. Lark searched the room. Surely she would have left a note if she'd decided to go back to her sister's. *Are you all out in the room?* He couldn't be sure when he'd last seen her. *It's with you online.* How could he escape from the eternity of commerce, the grammar of all things bought and sold? He scrambled for the remote. *Going, going ... for the last time are we all done? Any advance on...* The remote had disappeared. It was no wonder Aunt had gone out for one of her rare walks. Rest must have been impossible amidst this search for a bargain. How odd there was no way of switching off the television at the side; it didn't appear to be attached to the mains. *Gone. Sold to the man who came through on the ethernet.*

When he next looked up, the scene had moved from the auctioneer to the crowd. The last of the buyers and bidders were packing up and moving towards the back of the hall. The wooden chairs were empty, apart from one man seated in the front row and clad incongruously in a red dressing-gown, which Leonard saw for long enough to know it was identical to the one in the house. The camera alighted again on a presenter, lingering for a moment on his striped blazer and his full-faced, moustachioed bonhomie. The credits began to roll. The man in the dressing-gown stood up and moved towards the camera, a hand over his eyes as if he were trying to peer past the names of producers and editors descending in white block capitals.

Once again Leonard walked back through the house. There was no sign of a red dressing-gown draped over the banister. It was dawn now, livid but still tinged with blue, as if the night-bruise were fading into white skin; and high above, the faintest husks of cloud, hollowed out. He went through the back door and out onto the path to the shed. A keen wind shuffled the dry leaves. In the early morning light, the shed appeared less substantial; not a shadow anchored it to the ground. Then as he took out the key he was surprised to discover himself intensely certain, so convinced that any other outcome would have been an absurdity, that if he unlocked the door there could be nothing but empty space, colder than could ever have seemed possible, and everything stolen but the dust.

~

At six o'clock on the same morning, Aunt had been surprised to see the garden beckoning to her through the window. It was hardly light and yet she saw an enchantment forming under the branches of the birch tree, a silver occasion, as if only at this hour could the new day fascinate beyond the inevitable turn of the seasons. 'Everyday Antiques' was hiding behind a blank screen. Perhaps somewhere the cameras were still rolling—or was another programme waiting in the wings? Either way, it was a long time since she'd been out in the garden, especially at this hour. She put on her cardigan and took a stick from the umbrella stand. As she opened the French window, she'd heard a voice behind her and the unmistakably sound of a gavel striking wood. 'Everyday Antiques' must once more have resumed its progress through the hours. But she did not turn back. All her furniture had been sold: the gate-leg table she'd polished to a gleam; the what-not she'd inherited from her grandfather; the escritoire bought in the lanes of a city on the south coast; and fifty other ornaments and curios, each one a memento of an occasion in her long life.

She was on the path and turning onto the grass underneath the birch tree when she tripped and fell awkwardly, hearing the crack of her thin bones before she lost consciousness.

~

It was some time since Aunt had wandered off on her own, but as she had always returned Mr Lark saw no reason to forgo his early morning walk. Mrs N would soon be in. Impregnably reliable, she'd her own key to the front door and would be sure to look out for Aunt when she realised he wasn't back. The farmer was singing a hymn on the other side of the hedge, which appeared higher and greener. Although the words were familiar, there was something different about them today. 'Bright every morning will be the sun...' That was it! The tense had changed. If he didn't keep his head down, he would see the gate and then, for all he knew, he would find himself with the dog, in the future fields of someone else's experience. He watched the leaves drift across the road, the driest with a series of sharp clicks rising above the scuttle.

Aunt was not sure how long she'd been lying under the silver birch watching the sky brighten. Every inch of daylight falling sharpened her pain. She tried to move her legs but they were no longer taking instructions. If she turned her head to one side, she could see her stick, awry on the grass and just out of reach. She'd called out for Leonard more than once, but her voice was ancient and feeble. The garden had never seemed so large since she was a child.

~

Mrs N phoned, leaving a message on the answer machine. She had a bad cold and wouldn't in be today.

~

Wind skittered the leaves, which danced for a moment or brushed her motionless legs. Was the pain any worse? Possibly not but she was certain she was weakening now. It was strange to be so still under the birch where she played as a child; yet there was some consolation in sensing something greater than herself accumulating, gathering the power to entice from the roots of the silver tree. She'd been correct to intuit the imminence of an important event.

It was then that the man bent over her. He wore a suit the colour of dead leaves and was holding a white shroud, which a quirk of the light turned first flesh pink and then a vibrant red. So it couldn't be a shroud; it was far too jolly. But why shouldn't a shroud be cheerful? She tried to raise herself off the ground, but there was no need as the man was bending right over her, helping her into the garment. She'd seen him before—but where? 'Everyday Antiques'? Yes, of course. And he was gently helping her into a red dressing-gown, which fitted her so snugly. Not a shroud after all, but something curiously beautiful, almost uplifting. And wasn't it fine to be assisted by someone who'd been on the television! It was a shame there was no one about to share the moment. But at least in dying she had found the grace of her true elegance, the red dressing-gown that suited her best.

 SARAH PALEY

THE FOX CONDEMNS THE TRAP AND NOT HIMSELF

They buy exotic hens that lay fabulous
huge blue & green & speckled eggs. They
exclaim: *You can taste the colors!*

Fuck these low brows. Should have put in my
order though this would make an excellent story for
Xuanji. The tale of my magnificent tail – ouch –

caught by
ordinary
neighbors.
Damn them!
Every single
man, woman & child.
Nasty
species.

To be brought to
heel by such an in-
elegant genus.

Tomorrow –
regrets?
Absolutely
preposterous.

Alright then,
now. I
demand! I

need! I will
open this con-
traption!

Have a Heart –
inscribed on the
metal. Free &
sensical
expression is
lost on these
fiends.

 JENNY GRASSL

MAKING GRAPE CONSERVES

September is what I am cooking in the demon pot of suns,

so less and less of blue, skies spoiled in the grape

loosed from vine and thread, gone gobbledygook, attached

to the witch light of July—corkscrew, limbed acrobat

of seeking. Woody now, monument to my own falling.

I could save our vacation in post card gloss, toss

the spidering in the eaves. Or, dislodge the cottage furniture,

empty the rooms—funnel the ghouls into jars to preserve

their sight like the frog clear-eyed in his brine, cured

so we can poke and name his parts. Names for it all—

melancholia, this purpling browse, the ripe smell in the house.

Carolyn Guinzio

THEY ARE BUT SHADOWS
OF WHAT IS TO COME

The yet-to-be   strolled   along the sidewalk
          grabbing fistfuls   of jasmine   from the privacy
hedge   crushing fallen   apricots under
          their boots   alien earrings   hiding their eyes
shyly   in their necks   hills in the distance
          didn't arrest   the future   the way they arrested
the progress   of the rain-   heavy clouds.

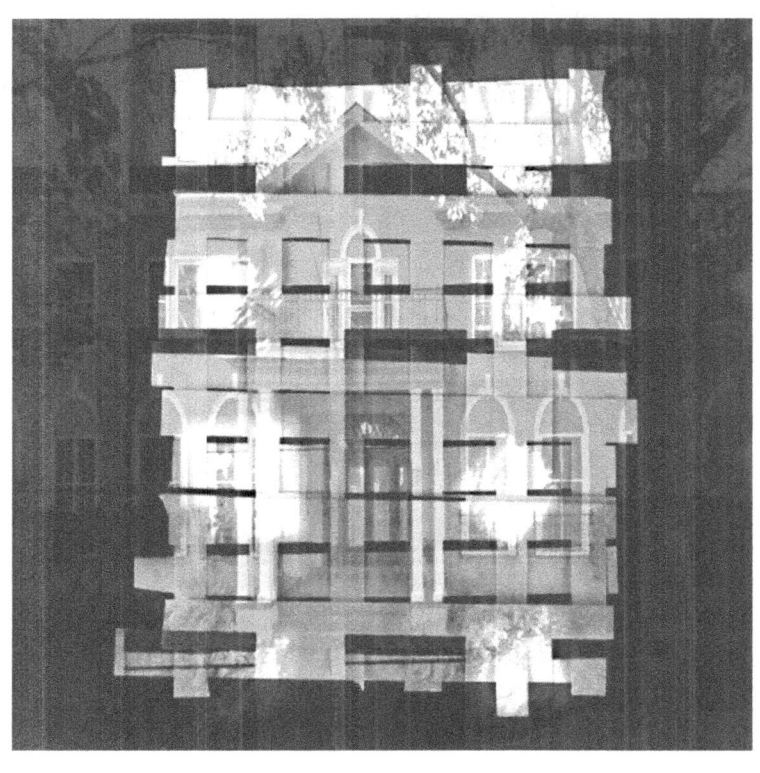

DANIEL M. JAFFE

TILTING ILANA

If you travel to Mexico City in September of 2013 as I did, you will wish to stay at La Casa del Conde in the Condesa neighborhood. Actually, they don't call them "neighborhoods" in Ciudad de México, known locally as *Distrito Federal*—D.F. (pronounced, 'Day Éfay'), but "*colonias*." So, technically, it's Colonia Condesa, but don't think it's some sort of tribute-paying colony of D.F., even though the ancient Aztecs held their empire together via a tribute system. Colonia Condesa is very much part of the city, the nicest part, you will say, unless you prefer pretentiously wealthy Colonia Polanco, in which case you're probably a snob who wouldn't be reading this travel guide article of mine anyway.

Rumor has it that Colonia Condesa once belonged to a countess—a *condesa* (duh)—who donated the territory to the city, so it became Colonia Condesa, whose historical ties to nobility enhance the attraction for would-be snobs lacking wealth. Tree-lined streets, residential three-four story buildings, grassy medians, an endless array of restaurants, cafés, bars, nightclubs, bookstores and shops, although not ritzy shops like you'll find in Polanco, especially on its Avenida Presidente Masaryk, named not for a countess but for a president—twentieth-century politicians deemed themselves the equivalent of historical nobility.

In many ways, there's no separation in D.F. of past and present, then and now and tomorrow, which is why you might well be able to visit when I did even though you'll be doing so at some future time. This notion of temporal fluidity can be attributed to the Aztec and Mayan calendar makers who were incredibly farsighted, predicting ends of millennial eras. For proof of my indisputable thesis, go to Pino Suarez metro station and gawk at the remains of an ancient Aztec pyramid dedicated to Ehecatl, the Aztec god of wind, on display exactly where it was unearthed in the late 1960's, smack in the middle of a metro station connecting the system's two busiest lines, proof indeed that the ancient Aztecs possessed incredible foresight, erecting this pyramid, as they did, precisely on the spot where their mystical priests (or alien guides from outer space) foresaw that a metro hub would be built half a millenium later, a locale maximizing the number of visitors streaming to pay homage throughout the ages. For the ancient

Aztecs, history was not just the past that had preceded, but also the future to come, with themselves as pivot point.

You won't have to plan tomorrow's breakfast if you stay, as I'm advising you to stay, at La Casa del Conde bed *and breakfast* on Calle Cholula. When the taxi drops you at La Casa del Conde for the first time, you'll ring the doorbell beside the nondescript door that looks like so much off-white metal sheeting, and will be greeted by Ilana. Say hello from me. She'll remember me unless she's forgotten. You'll know she's Ilana because she'll be the woman greeting you. Only Ilana will greet you, whether you arrive at 7 AM or 6 PM or midnight or 3 AM. Like an Aztec calendar, she is reliably there round the clock, presumably has always been there and always will be. She will give a warm, albeit tentative, "Hello" in English and will take a step back to give you space to carry your luggage into the patio, which is actually an enclosed former driveway masquerading as entrance foyer. You'll look at Ilana's long pretty face, chestnut brown waist-length hair, and will observe her shapely petite figure, but what you'll notice most about Ilana is that she'll be tilting. Your first inclination will be to dismiss her tilting as a consequence of the entire city having been built first by the Aztecs and then by Cortés on a lake, on artificial islands— *chinampas*—of mud and decaying vegetation. You'll have read that buildings in *el centro histórico* of the city tilt, so you'll think that tilting is normal. But then you'll notice this patio's floor to be quite level. Furthermore, you'll realize that you are not tilting, that only Ilana is tilting.

She'll be wearing a skirt-length turtleneck sweater over tight jeans, and as she turns to lead you into the building, she'll tug down the sweater's hem as if to cover her shapely behind and distract from her pronounced limp. Please ask her right then and there whether she suffered polio as a child, or whether one of her legs is shorter than the other. I've been wondering about this a great deal since my trip, never having been so rude as to ask, but if you'd ask, I'd be most grateful. Kindly write this mystery's answer to me in care of the publisher of this travel guide you're reading.

After recording your passport number and imprinting your credit card for payment for your upcoming entire two-week stay (as mentioned above, Aztecs are forward-looking), Ilana will point out the breakfast room beside the foyer. Seated behind her desk during that welcome encounter, Ilana will initially come across as meek, and you'll feel sorry for her because of her limp, which you'll assume must make dating a challenge because who'd want to date a defective? You'll be embarrassed by your own thoughts, as well you should be. In fact, you'll attribute loneliness to be the reason she's forever waiting in the lobby, as if desperate for company from any source at any hour. You may be right. Or, you might regard her as a seventeenth-century disciple of the nun Sor Juana, drawn through time by the exigencies of the present to bring lessons of humility and contemplation to our age, at least as far future as September 2013, which is when I'm encouraging you to schedule your trip because I cannot speak with authority about D.F. after that time.

From her seat behind a desk which keeps you at a respectable distance from her tight yet shapely figure, Ilana will describe which of the four rooms at the top of the stairs is yours.

"A steep staircase," you'll comment.

"Aztec tradition," she'll reply, adding with a scowl, "You homosexuals are such curious people."

You will be nonplussed by her assertion, both by its content and the fact that she chose to state it to you, but then you'll realize she probably attempts to knock everyone off balance psychologically the way she feels off balance physically, an effort on her part to level the playing field that is social interaction. For Ilana, life's one big soccer match with ego as the ball. The only question is who gets to kick whose ball first, hardest, and farthest in order to score. (As you may know, the ancient Aztecs played *ullamaliztli*, a pre-soccerish game they knew would one day evolve into present-day *fútbol*, which might well currently be evolving into something else.)

In response to Ilana's let's-face-it rude prying into your sexual proclivities, you might be tempted to protest too much that she's mistaken because this is a foreign country and what if they butcher homosexuals here? (They generally don't, but you might not know that.) So, take the prudent approach and hold your tongue so that no one cuts it out.

For obvious reasons, Ilana won't lead you upstairs to your room with its bed but no dresser. Strange plastic green-white-purple vines will dangle in each of the room's four corners as decoration on blindingly white walls. These plastic flora will remind of what you stuck in your turtle's tank as a boy, thinking he'd never notice the difference between plastic and living plant flesh. You will notice the difference.

After settling in and showering—you must shower because Mexicans in D.F. are notoriously clean and well-groomed—ask Ilana for a map, and ask her to circle the Patriotismo metro station. Although Ilana's map marking will be accurate, don't expect to find the metro station easily: the D.F. metro station entrance signs are completely obscured by blue or red tarpaulin-covered food and vendor stalls constituting informal mini-malls (to use a chauvinistic domestic reference you're likely to grasp) selling freshly griddled green *nopal*-flour tacos, *tortas* (buns) stuffed with chicken or meat with aromatic garlic and onions, fresh-squeezed juices and fresh-cut mangoes, kiwis, prickly pears, watermelons, cantaloupes, as well as costume earrings and bracelets, pens, paper pads, and anything else useful. Another day, you will see at the Museo Nacional de Antropología in Bosque Chapultepec (think Central Park), a diorama of the ancient Aztec market known as *El Mercado en Tlatelolco*, a market remarkably reminiscent of contemporary metro station markets. This constitutes further proof of Aztec foresight when we consider that they, who knew nothing of subway travel, designed their markets with the obvious intent of inspiring future generations to surround metro station entrances with markets. Amazing.

Once you discover the hidden Patriotismo metro entrance, descend the broad staircase and wait on the platform. Be sure, if it's rush hour and you're a man (you are a man, aren't you?), not to enter the first few cars, which will be reserved exclusively for women and children so as to protect them from the shovings and gropings of us men aka pigs in any culture. Presumably, you will not be so foolish as to travel by metro at rush hour, so you'll be spared the excessive testosterone flow that impels men here to turn every group encounter into a *Lucha Libre* wrestling match.

Travel four stations to Chabacano, exit, walk through the maze to the line that will take you to Pino Suarez, exit, spend time in this station admiring the aforementioned Ehecatl pyramid and scolding yourself for imagining that every limping woman—the young one in a long skirt and pushing a stroller, the middle-aged woman with freshly coiffed hair, the hobbling old woman in a shawl—is Ilana, because that would be impossible, and an example, you will tell yourself, of your own prejudices at play. Spend a good ten minutes figuring out how to exit the station, then do so and ask with a dumb expression, "Zócalo?"

As you walk along Avenida Pino Suarez, be sure to stop and examine the enormous wall carving that marks the spot where, in the sixteenth-century, Moctezuma and Cortés first met. Right along Pino Suarez, one of the central shopping avenues in modern Mexico City. Don't tell me the Aztecs didn't select that spot on purpose. Don't tell me they didn't know that future generations would commemorate this historic meeting with a wall carving legible from across a wide *avenida* smack in the middle of future entrepreneurial Mexico.

Continue walking until you reach the Zócalo, the historic center of the Aztec and colonial Spanish worlds, where you'll encounter a disgusting tent city of teachers from around the country come to strike against new legislation demanding that they pass qualifying exams and cease selling their teaching licenses to unqualified others. As you'll see locals do, cover your mouth with a handkerchief and hold your nose as you pass the rows of turquoise porta-potties, and abandon all hope of entering the Palacio Nacional with its Diego Rivera murals and other splendors you'll never get to see because it's closed on account of the sit-in beside it. Just keep walking to the plaza's far corner to the ancient Aztec Templo Mayor. Don't be stingy, pay to wander the archeological grounds because they're a marvel with carved serpents and a series of stone walls, a (replica) wall of skulls, and remnants of broad, steep staircases vaguely reminiscent of those metro station stairs you just climbed down—another example of Aztec foresight regarding metro stations. Take photos in order to see these ruins come alive in your camera's viewfinder: the stone serpents will writhe, the stone walls will drip blood, the skulls will issue chilling screams in the loveliest counterpoint.

Spend time gazing at the engaging *chacmool*, a polychrome sculpted figure reclining and holding a huge bowl on his belly. As you observe him—knees bent, upper body inclining up—you will surely agree with my assessment that he looks caught by surprise mid-stomach-crunch. Which naughty no-no was he doing that his turned, staring-right-at-you face now bears an expression of surprise or even guilt? Did he yank the bowl over his belly and crotch with his left hand because he was doing something lascivious with his right? And are the speculations of other guidebooks accurate that the bowl is meant for peaceful offerings to the god Tláloc? Or am I right that the bowl would perfectly hold a human head? One man's peace offering is another man's decapitation. Watch through your camera's viewfinder and hear him giggle.

Be sure, too, to spend lots of time in the Templo's museum where you'll see all sorts of fascinating historical artifacts, most notably an enormous stone disc carving of dismembered Coyolxauhqui, who led an attack of 400 siblings against their mother, Coatlicue, the fecund Mother of the Gods. This daughter, Coyolxauhqui, was vanquished and dismembered by her mother's newest child, the sun god, Huitzilopochtli, sprung fully armed from her belly. Coyolxauhqui appears decapitated on this enormous stone disc relief, a skull at her side, her arms and legs dismembered, her breasts bare. Most fascinating are the laser light beams from above that cast onto the relief rainbow reproductions of ancient coloration divined from pigments discovered in the stone itself: blue, white, red, ochre. Modern science illuminates the ancient history that ultimately led, through centuries of perambulation, to the modern science. This circular stone disc will remind you of the circular Aztec calendar.

You'll definitely wish to take lots of photographs of the Catedral Metropolitana beside the Templo. Spaniards hauled stones from the Templo (rather, their Aztec slaves did the hauling) in order to build this cathedral, another example of ancient Aztec foresight: building their temple with precisely the sorts of stones the Spaniards could later use to construct a Baroque and Neo-Classical cathedral, a dramatically different architectural conceptualization. Be prepared, when gazing at the Catedral through your viewfinder, to hear its stones shriek shrill agony. Note the stench of rotting flesh. Set the camera aside and the stench will dissipate.

This will have been quite enough for one day, so you should return to La Casa del Conde guesthouse via whichever metro station remains open that particular day in September 2013 depending on the fancy of El Presidente, a more whimsical fellow than the electorate had anticipated. Upon your return, tilting Ilana will ask what you saw and will lecture, "No tourist can see more than fragments that will later blend in memory to create a coherent vision of past experience. It's all a question of discovering the right pieces, which is impossible for you to do because you know nothing of the city, so listen to me." She will inquire as to your plans for tomorrow, will dismiss them as a waste of time and will arrange for a private driver to show you the charming neighborhood of Coayacan.

Next morning, skip lengthy conversation with Ilana by acknowledging that you'd best eat quickly so as to be on time for the driver. Ilana will nod and insist upon posing one question as you slip past her into the breakfast room: "Did you dream about me?"

Realizing now that Ilana had, in fact, invaded your dreams—a long-haired limping dragon breathed fire and singed your genitals—you'll grimace. She'll grin.

Eat your *chilaquiles* (think nachos with tomato sauce and tasteless feta) quickly and thank limping Josefina, the cook.

Your driver, who will look remarkably like a male version of Ilana, will take you to charming Coayacan, to Frida Kahlo's Casa Azul house museum that you'll photograph in all its indigo blue blue blue glory. Examine the home's indigenous Mexican ceramics and antique furniture, fancily dressed skeletons, and a huge courtyard displaying cacti, yucca, palms, small sculptures, as well as a red and yellow mini-temple mount. Wandering through, you will enter the room displaying Frida's many corsets, at which point you will recall the pain the woman so frequently (constantly?) suffered, and her difficulty walking at times, the consequences of a bus accident in which her spine was broken, her foot was crushed, and her uterus was pierced by a handrail, which latter horror threatened the womanhood she obsessively spent the rest of her life trying to assert by engaging in sex with every man and woman she could seduce.

Frida was, you might surmise, selected by fertile Mother Goddess Coatlicue for continuation of her mythical daughter's disfigured Mexican womanness, Frida as Coatlicue's rebellious daughter in modern times, a Mexican woman glorifying the past with implements of the present, dressing the way Coatlicue's pueblo contemporaries might have dressed, spawning and disseminating the feel of Mexico's essence to the world. Ironically, so as to assure Frida's continuity and prevent her downfall, Coatlicue protected Frida from ever bearing children who could turn on her and try to kill her.

The driver will return you to the guesthouse where Ilana will be waiting to learn of your impressions.

"Worth every peso," should be your only response.

"Tomorrow," she'll instruct, "return to *el centro histórico*. Tomorrow. Be sure tomorrow."

"Because...?"

"Tomorrow. Not a different day. Tomorrow." She'll turn her back to you and you'll shrug and conclude that mystery is part of Mexico, so—tomorrow.

Tomorrow you'll sleep late, miss breakfast, and then slip out while Ilana cleans the breakfast room. Return downtown, poke through various shops along Avenida 5 de Mayo and end up at the Casa de los Azulejos, "House of Blue Tiles," a building covered, as you might surmise, in blue tiles, offering a cohesive vision composed of fractures in blue tile and white stucco. Be sure to take a photo because as you look through your camera's viewfinder, the building's blues will appear more vibrant than when seen with the naked eye, will appear to be a series of afternoon sky patches tugged by artisan fingertips from the sky and affixed here for earthly delight. They will dance and shift, these sky patches, exchanging places from high to low, left to right.

Here you'll lunch at a Sanborns chain restaurant in a grandiose, Baroque-Moorish balconied dining room with marble-squared floors, two-story concrete pillars, and a yellow, peacock-featuring mural that covers an entire wall and bears a tile-framed fountain at its center. The *cochinita pibil* (too piquant a sweet-and-sour for your taste in pork, but you're here to experience) will be brought by your limping waitress who resembles an Ilana in typical Sanborns campy white-bodiced dress with phony-looking, brightly colored, triangular yoked arts-and-craftsy multi-color-striped skirt. Shame on Sanborns for making history hokey. She'll even sound like Ilana when she takes your order in clipped authoritarian tones, and she'll look at you with Ilana's signature mix of amusement and disdain.

Tip her well just in case she actually is who she cannot possibly be.

Leave the gorgeous Azulejos building, then continue down Avenida 5 de Mayo. Because you're there on September 5, 2013 as Ilana (and I) instructed, you'll hear the beat of drums in the distance. Crane your neck to see hundreds of near-naked men. Make a beeline for them. Climb up the portico stairs of a corner building so as to look out at the crowd crossing Avenida Lázaro Cárdenas back and forth at every change of traffic light. They'll be marching, dancing to drumbeats:

Ba-ba-bum

Ba-ba-bum

Ba-ba-ba-ba-ba-ba-bum.

Over and over. And chanting, "*Au-dien-cia*," with emphasis on the last syllable. Audience. You are their audience, but that's not why they're demonstrating.

Hundreds and hundreds of men in briefs or boxers, socks and shoes or boots. Men from their 20's to their 70's. Many in straw hats, many without. All of chocolatl complexion although none with particularly interesting physiques—a disappointment if I were attracted to men, which I'm not, although you, the reader of this gay guidebook, might well be. Each of these men will have covered his crotch (also a disappointment if I were...but I'm not...but you may well be...) with a dangling sheet of paper, a flier bearing the face of one or another government leader and stating, "*Represor*" or "*Discriminación*." Take many photos and, while peering through your camera's viewfinder, watch this horde suddenly wield obsidian knives, hear them chant in some language other than Spanish, observe as their briefs and boxers become loincloths.

A limping woman who looks like Ilana, except in white blouse instead of turtleneck, will be collecting donations. Toss a few pesos in payment for the right to gawk. She will also pass out fliers—"*Movimiento de los 400 Pueblos*"—explaining that these are *campesinos* (peasant farmers) demanding an audience with the *Secretario de Gobernación* on agrarian reforms. They're also protesting alleged discrimination by the chief of D.F. police. They say they've been trying to get an audience for a year now, and that the men are naked because they feel stripped of rights and identity. The number 400 should resonate for you. The demonstration continues for an entire block, down around the corner of Avenida Lázaro Cárdenas and Avenida Benito Juárez, both streets named for past leaders who gave rights to the *campesinos*. Note the stories-high banner hanging on a building and depicting the *Secretario de Gobernación* in a Darth Vader helmet. Hollywood in history used by these near naked *campesinos* to appeal to the conscience of the past in efforts to achieve a liveable future. Does time fold like a curtain? Can ordinary men pierce several folds in a single glance?

Take a stroll past the the white marble, Art Deco, Palacio de Bellas Artes, which will be closed at that particular moment, continue through the adjoining Parque Alameda Central, beautiful with its paths, classical statues, and beds of agapanthus blue starbursts. Your attention will surely be grabbed by the dancing fountain with criss-crossing jet sprays reminiscent of your pre-adolescence when you had peeing contests with your best friend and neighbor. (You are a man, aren't you?)

At this point, you might be wondering why I accepted a writing assignment for a gay travel guidebook—after all, I'm not gay. Well, travel-writing gigs are few and far between nowadays, and gays like to travel, so.... Besides, I always loved Tijuana where I could get Viagra cheaply and without prescription, not that I need it, but I'm hoarding for my old age. Fortunately, something about me prompted a sparkle in my editor's eye—my androgynous lankiness? My dyed-blue buzz cut? The "I Love Lucy" tattoo on my right forearm? After assigning the gig, he made a pass. Not wishing to mislead, I turned him down with "I'm not gay." He replied, "Seriously?" Nevertheless, he let me keep the assignment.

All this talk of gayness is relevant because I'm about to describe the gay plaque you'll encounter after you exit the Parque Alameda and head toward the José Martí community center building. There it will hang right in front of you, a plaque commemorating a November 1901 assault on dancing gays, some of whom were wearing women's clothes. You can picture this thanks to a cartoon caricature of the event you will see another day in the Museo Nacional de Arte: among other newspaper broadsheets by José Guadalupe Posada, you'll see his rendering of dancing men—some dressed in tuxes and others, with mustaches, in hour-glass figure-fitting evening gowns. It will be entitled "*41 Maricones*," "41 Faggots."

Be sure to photograph this commemorative plaque because you'll enjoy the sensation of looking through the viewfinder to see yourself participating in the revelry there and then, yourself dressed in corsetted, puffy-sleeved bodice and long skirt, your mustache waxed to fine points, your gaze fixed on that of your tuxedoed male escort waltzing you away from the present moment of fear and repression into a fantasy time, what will become an actual future time, distant, when you and he will cease to be the object of derision, but of well-wishing rice throwers, of professional photographers and caterers eager for your legislatively legitimized business.

As you set down your camera and turn from the plaque, you will likely notice a handsome suited man grinning, so you'll give a nod because that's the polite thing to do, and will go on your way, but he'll likely follow because some Mexicans are sex-starved. To dissuade further unwanted attention, take out your camera and aim its lens at him. He'll do a heel-toe spin and reverse course, which defensive behavior will confirm your suspicion of his nefarious intentions despite his high-cheekboned, strong-nosed, broadly smiling face.

Easy for him to misunderstand your intentions because the plaque is located practically around the corner from a contemporary gay cruising ground—how insightful of those 41 Faggots in 1901 to hold their dance right there, just around the corner from what would become a cruising ground a hundred years thence. As you stroll through the Plaza de la Solidaridad where my editor told me to "watch your *culito*," you will think his remark ridiculous because it's a manicured, wide-open plaza with no apparent place for men to go grabbing one another's asses unless they step into the WC smack in the center of the plaza or into the Starbucks across the avenue or the neighboring Hilton, which certainly would be doable if one could afford a room there. (I couldn't because my editor's a cheapskate.)

In the Plaza, you'll spot a sculpture of a flagless pole being grasped by three giant bronze gray-green fists which will appear, through your camera's viewfinder, to be moving rhythmically up and down the pole. You will find this somewhat suggestive and wonder which was established first—the park's cruisiness or its sculpture. You'll also see men playing chess.

The plaza will be broken up by benches into several small squares surrounding fountains, some of which will spout suggestively white foamy water and some of which will not. You'll sit on one of those green-painted metal benches and, if you happen to be writing an article for a gay book or magazine, you'll jot down observations. In no time flat, a white-haired man with black-framed glasses will sit at the end of your bench. He'll open his beige backpack, pull out an iPhone, plug in earbuds and will pay you no mind whatsoever, a very clever ruse designed to make you think he has no interest in you.

Then a young fellow with wavy black hair, blue tee-shirt, jeans, and newish gray running shoes will sit on a bench positioned at a 90-degree angle to yours. He'll look remarkably like a male version of Ilana, but without a limp. No matter how many times you wink at him, he will not return your glance, will just take some book out of his bright blue backpack and read—or pretend to. Apparently, accepted Mexican cruising behavior is to appear not to be cruising at all.

A mere two feet from this Ilana-impersonating young fellow, a middle-aged man with a big head and a blue oxford shirt saying "Quick Learning" above his pocket will sit and examine the back of a package that states, in English, "Rat Poison." He, too, will ignore your glances, a sure sign he is self-consciously harboring deep interest.

In a few moments, he will stand and leave without blowing you so much as a kiss. Then the white-haired man with earbuds will stand and leave. As will the blue tee-shirted young fellow. All three will cross Avenida Benito Juárez and walk out of sight around the corner. You will be perplexed. And envious, not that you would join them in anything but curious fantasy.

After all this time, you will need to use the WC—pay your five pesos to the Ilana look-alike lady who asks if you want "*papel*," which you may or may not think you need, but you should nonetheless take in hand. You'll walk left to the men's room where you'll see a youngish man primping his hair in the chipped mirror. He'll look at you and smile. You'll ignore him and go into a stall with very low doors and toilet but no seat—you'll be thankful you took the toilet paper wad. When you step out of the stall, he'll still be there primping, looking your way and smiling, and you'll be tempted out of curiosity, although not desire. Flee his breach of mustn't-be-obvious cruising etiquette.

As reward for your common sense and restraint, you will see a woman identical to Ilana except in ways that she's not. She will be thin with a dark, high-cheekboned triangular Asiatic face. Straight black hair parted down the middle and pulled back into a long, waist-length pony tail. You'll know she's an Indian because she'll be dressed not unlike the way Frida Kahlo dressed in an effort to look indigenous: a dark green blouse with puffy half sleeves tied tight above each elbow. White trim on her yolk. Big orange bead necklace on a brown cord. Ground-length loose white skirt with small orange and red flowers and green leaves growing from a magenta band around her hem. Two thin bracelets on each arm, one white and one turquoise. She'll hold a black cloth bag embroidered with big white flowers. Big black knit balls will dangle from the bag's bottom corners.

Seeing this even without looking through your camera's viewfinder, you'll be curious as to which truths the camera might reveal, so you'll step over to ask permission to photograph, but she'll slap you so hard you'll feel the sting the rest of the day. Then she'll spin and depart.

Perplexed and in pain, return to the refuge of the guesthouse and go to sleep.

The next day, your last, will be your final chance to stroll through Bosque Chapultepec, the above-mentioned wealthy Colonia Polanco, the incredible Museo Nacional de Antropología, and the good-but-ain't-no-Prado Museo Nacional de Arte, each of which exploration could fill an entire afternoon if not a day, so don't dawdle.

Return, exhausted, to the guesthouse where Ilana will ask, "Have you tried elote?"

"Elote?"

"Our version of your North American corn on the cob. White corn. Big kernels. To serve it, vendors shove a huge wooden skewer up the cob and slather on mayonnaise that drips. You'd probably like it."

"Sounds messy."

"Is that what's been holding you back?"

You'll stare, uncertain whether the implications are, indeed, the implications.

"It's your last night. Why did you choose to leave tomorrow, on Independence Day?"

"Prescience," you will say in admiration of ancient Aztec example.

"You should eat Mexican seafood," she'll say seemingly apropos of nothing. "I know a place. I'll call us a taxi."

"But if you dine with me," you'll ask in all obliviousness, "who'll man the reception desk?"

She'll stare with a puzzled look, then will reply, "After all you've experienced, you still haven't opened your mind to the possible?"

Take the three-minute drive with her to Avenida Nuevo Leon, where, on September 15, 2013, they'll serve you complimentary *amuses bouches* of *caldo de camarones*—shrimp broth with spice—and a tuna dip with chips. They'll encourage you to order their variation on delicious *chile en nogada*, the stuffed pepper dish everyone specializes in during this independence-day season, but Ilana will refuse to order something so typical because she wants dinner to be special for you, an odd lapse in her understanding that Mexican typicality *is* special for you. Let her order the *ceviche de pulpo*, which will be just chewy enough yet neither rubbery nor too vinegary. Then enjoy the *filete de pescado al mezcal con arroz* which will be sensational with a light flavor you won't be able to identify (*mezcal*, duh). Be sure to follow the advice of Sophia the waitress and indulge in one of the most amazing desserts of your life: *souffle de elote*, a corn souffle served with *dulce de leche* sauce and sides of vanilla ice cream, toasted nuts, and (whisky?) cream sauce.

Ilana will become enraged at the way you smile at Sophia, which will make no sense, since Ilana will be Sophia—not that you will realize the identicality until Sophia moans orgiastically each time Ilana takes a bite of dessert.

"I fell in love with you from the first," Ilana will admit then and there, reaching across the table and wiping with her thumb a drop of cream sauce from the left corner of your lower lip.

You'll be flabbergasted.

"I've been watching you every day," she'll continue. "Haven't you realized?"

Epiphany: "You were all the limping women in the metro that first day?"

"I was."

"And the woman handing out brochures at the demonstration of the 400?"

"Yes."

"And the waitress at Sanborns?"

She'll nod.

"And some of those men?"

Her eyes will widen gleefully.

"And the woman manning the WC?"

"I sold you paper to protect your *culito*."

"And the Indian woman who slapped?"

"I enjoyed that."

"Wow," you'll say, "that's impressive."

"I am impressive. So now will you take me to bed?"

You'll insist on paying the bill first, a delaying tactic. Lovely as she is, you'll wonder if you'd be compromising your gay-travel writer credentials if you were to bed a woman while on assignment, assuming, of course, that you're a non-gay, gay-travel writer like me.

To distract, you'll ask during the taxi ride back to La Casa del Conde, "But if you've been following me, who was minding the guesthouse?"

"Why do you assume I can be in only one place at a time…just because you can be in only one place at a time? Why project your limitations onto me?"

You'll remind her that you still have to pack for your flight tomorrow, so you'll thank her for dinner and head upstairs alone, listening to her frustrated stomps around the lobby.

Pack, then shower and spend the rest of the evening wearing nothing but briefs and reclining on pillows against the white wall, your knees bent up with laptop on belly so you can make final notes. At some point, you'll hear a resounding clomp clomp clomp up those steep steps, the uneven clomp of one strong foot and one weak, followed by a moment of silence and then, as you freeze in minor disbelief, you will detect the rattling of a key in your doorknob. You will call out, "Excuse me!"

Your door will fling open and Ilana will stand there in all her tilting glory, in boots but nothing else—no turtleneck, no jeans, no brassiere, no panties—and you will be sitting there: knees propped up with laptop on your belly, head turned, face staring in stupefaction.

"Just look at you," she'll remark in appreciation, "posing like one of our ancients." You'll make a mental note to figure out her reference, but at that moment, you'll be shocked by the advance of this naked and shapely woman who climbs onto your bed, yanks the laptop aside, rubs you through your briefs and exclaims with a smile, "So you're not gay, are you? I love being wrong."

Tomorrow on the airplane home, you will wonder at her (and your editor's) assumptions, but at this moment, you'll be thankful that you're experiencing joy as she swings her full-length left leg over you and mounts and rides (albeit with a tilt), all the while snapping her head from side to side, flailing her long chestnut hair, your hands instinctually reaching to grasp her breasts so firm they could be the pecs of an overworked-out muscle man, which overlay of images induces your hips to buck in rhythm with hers. You both exclaim yelps of climax.

You reach to pull her down in embrace, but she slides off you, says, "Thanks, I needed that," as if you were a cold Dos Equis on a hot day, and as suddenly as she arrived, she now departs, shutting the door closed behind. A slow clomp clomp clomp downstairs.

You stare at the purple, green, and white plastic vines dangling from the corners of your white-walled room, you scent the lingering aroma of her, wonder if this is the typical Mexican way between women and men, or whether you imagined the entire encounter, whether Ilana never left her desk downstairs at all or is some incarnation of a goddess of lasciviousness and joy, whether she'll expect you to extend your stay now that you've become lovers, or perhaps she uses all male guests this way? (You are male, aren't you?)

You'll dutifully shut your laptop, slip it into your backpack beside the packed suitcase against the wall. Without washing Ilana off or dabbing the messy wet sheets dry or pursuing her downstairs (as if you've the energy), you'll drift to sleep while fuzzily altering your sense of this woman you thought forever destined to remain at the bottom of the guesthouse stairs, hoping for yourself that your masculinity is what inspired Ilana to overcome the disability of history that masks itself as destiny, prompting her to prove herself capable of ascending to the highest of human heights.

Next morning, lugging your luggage, you'll hobble downstairs to the lobby, your lower body bruised and sore so that you'll limp a bit. Ilana will glare as if to despise your mockery which is not mockery, just the aftermath of tough love.

"Sleep well?" she'll ask, raising a sardonic eyebrow.

"Like the dead," which will be true.

The doorbell.

"Your taxi," she'll say, standing, stepping through the door to the entrance patio and unlocking the gate.

"My bags are here," you'll call out to the driver, and after he takes them, you'll ask Ilana for a farewell photograph as memento.

"Sentimentality will be your downfall," she'll prophesy, but she'll consent, will wheel her desk chair to the foot of the steep Mexican staircase where she'll sit, cross her legs and tilt her head because Ilana always tilts. You'll frame the shot, and as you look through the viewfinder you'll see not the young lady in turtleneck and jeans, but a vision confirming your previous suspicion: dismembered woman pieces suspended in proximate location to where limbs and other parts should be. You'll hesitate, then will nevertheless click because you'll wish to retain for tomorrow this proof that you've been here and part of this place, these days, these people, everyone who's been here, and who will be.

 Jack e Lorts

EPHRAM PRATT SURRENDERS
TO SURREALISM

A   n ordinary
man   cultivating

is   not unlike
cut   ting grass

in   to a warm day
half   of which is living

by   the worms of nature,
a   mountain of sand

win   nowing in sadness,
dow   agers sleeping

a   nd rejecting knowledge
man   kind knows

is   not violable as is
cut   ting grass

in   an organdy glass
half   full of vapor, swung

by   closets closing doors
a   nd knots tied to

win   d sox absconding
dow   n empty stairs

GREGORY KIMBRELL

THE FLESH IS A THING TO BE REMOVED.

Grete's brother believed that a horn was growing from his forehead. He could sense it just beneath the skin, where, so he said, a stag beetle had made an incision with its serrated mandibles and crawled inside. Of course, a number of stag beetles and other omnivorous insects made nests in the area at this time of year, but if there was now an abnormally large population, then this was no cause to dream up a condition hitherto unknown to science.

One night, Grete woke up when
something tickled her chest. She
brushed it to the floor and saw, by
the light of the cold moon, a stag
beetle. She put her drinking glass
upside down on top of it, then fell
back into a deep sleep. But when
morning came, the glass was empty.
Had she half-dreamed what took
place only a few hour before? As
she unbuttoned her nightgown, she
discovered a neat slash across the
front, as though it had been cut with
scissors.

She took a bowl of creamed rice to her brother, who had a fever, but he had wrapped himself so tightly in the bedclothes that none of his body was visible. She opened the windows to dissipate the stale odor in the room. No one was out strolling. Grete always felt like the city, at this hour, belonged to her alone. The day ahead was hers also, and anything was possible. She put her hand on the cocoon-like bundle lying on the bed, but there was no one inside it.

People around the city had begun to disappear. On Thursday, Margaret said, Today will be my day to leave. Grete asked, Are you in some kind of trouble? Margaret said, Who isn't? I may not be sprouting antlers or wings, but since when are they necessary for disappearing? They're only pretexts. Grete did not understand. Was disappearing not the same as killing oneself or running away? But if this city had its problems, then so did anyplace else that she knew of. People must be losing their minds.

Your day will come, Margaret said. On Friday, she was not in school. So, for the first time in years, Grete walked home alone. As she passed Margaret's house, she saw, by the gate, Margaret's cat. Beneath its paw lay a splendid specimen of the sphinx moth, dead. The population of the school had already fallen by nearly half. The halls were quieter between classes. But while it was true that some pleasant girls were gone, so too were some who been a real nuisance.

Perhaps they all had been monsters at heart and deserved disappearing. Perhaps monstrousness could lie dormant and unobservable in a soul and rise up suddenly to consume it. Grete, however, was no monster. She was too apt to see the beauty in things. As she looked across the empty schoolyard, the breeze scattered the smoke rising from the incinerator. It was a splendid day, and she felt herself lifted above the world, into the clear, life-giving sunshine.

ADRIAN BLEVINS

STATUS QUO

Status Quo wanted to try a séance—to sit in the dark with the soundly dead. She wanted to have a wolf maybe love her, and for her love it really back, and for each one to lick the other's face. She imagined him with her and her with him and a leash and color of supple red leather, a mountain they could climb. Status Quo wanted to eat a squid dipped in spiced mayo. Maybe chili peppers and mustard, maybe kale or something more clandestine from the not-fetid waters of maybe 'Nam. She sat wherever she was and thought of her wanting as a kind of mist that was more like smog or RAID or MSG that she wanted to tag like a toe in the morgue so she'd be better prepared next time.

*

Status Quo could not wrap her head around football, so she went to the library to study the vocabulary. On the way she bought a dark blue jersey. She put it on and took off her panties. But then she put them right back on again.

*

Status Quo loved tennis and tennis balls and tennis courts and nets and nets and nets and nets and nets.

*

Status Quo liked shopping when the weather was good—certain legendary boutiques. Status Quo did not like shopping in the rain. She did not like sleet or any kind of very tiny even hurricane. She didn't like to sweat, either, except if perspiration was called for as it obviously was when she was on the treadmill with her headband on.

*

Status Quo had a nightmare. It could have been lurid. It might have involved her car. There might be a scratch on something right now—a rub, a nick, a cut, a scrape, a scruff. Status Quo said to nobody in particular that it was just too dark to see.

*

Status Quo dipped her head in a bowl of lemons. So as to attempt to alleviate the darkening. She would have tired peroxide but feared the slutty yellow. Status Quo ironed her pencil skirt. She decided to apply for a job at A Quarter Till Eight, which she hoped was not a bar or a café, but a bank. She shook her one good pen two times. Three. Four. The heart of Status Quo was shaking then, like a real quake.

 JOHN GARMON

THE LIGHT THAT FALLS

A glance of sun fires the tenure of trees.
It is lost in the scurrying feelers of crabs.
It cracks under the flat rock propped by the dune.
Heavy winds drive clouds down its burning throat.
Then the mist comes as if created from solid earth.
Across prairies there are howling calls of fault.
Tornadoes try to pay for what the light conveys.
The light sucks up the earth as cargo and renames it.
All this ugly and beautiful strength from a fire in space.

It skips rope with children at recess at school.
They look at it through fragile flesh of fingers.
It grows in their bodies until they are old and thick.
Then it snaps its fingers and flees and they die.
They go down into the earth still warm from the light.
They carry its message until their bones are free.

 SUSAN DEFREITAS

METAMORPHOSIS NO. 1

My work is a game, a very serious game.
                                        –M. C. Escher

A door with a brass handle in a long hallway creaks open; inside is a faded Oriental rug and a lazy lion, who looks up.

It is a room of full of colors, masks moving, a masquerade. Bare breasts elevated to nervous heights above tittering laughter and the memory of music. Through the window, the Atlantic stretches and yawns.

But maybe not. Maybe it's only two children, making believe in a seaside attic. The girl giggling from behind a fan, flirting with the bust of a mannequin. The pert bosom of that Elizabethan maiden is revealed, in fact, as the young girl's apple cheeks; the gentleman's brass-handled riding crop, merely her brother's tousled cowlick.

The lazy lion, in this case, would double as the rug, losing its colors. Its head a kind of mask, mouth stretched wide—that fearsome roar, reduced to a yawn.

Then again, it wasn't necessarily an attic—it looked as if someone had opened a diner in a library. The young girl could just as easily have been a waitress. Maybe she was pouring coffee for a handsome man, eating apple pie. Maybe his face seemed oddly immobile, like a mask, until he looked up at her and smiled.

Was it the memory of laughter that moved him? Or did the bust of the waitress remind him, maybe, of some Elizabethan maiden in a painting he'd studied in school?

She looked a bit wistful, so far inland. Who's to say she didn't dream of the sea? Who's to say the man's childish cowlick didn't remind her a bit of her brother, a Leo, who'd shipped out to the Middle East?

The ceiling fan turns lazily above them, and between them, a great gulf yawns. He's making believe he's an artist. Inside her, the ocean roars.

SARA MOORE WAGNER

WITCH'S MARK

After I stop
shaking, you might find me
filled with holes,
my wrists, punctured
cans, the palms
of my hands: I've been pulled
out of the brambles, pierced.
Maybe you'll want to know how
like a mouth this body,
how the soles of my feet
carry me despite
the missing parts, how the blood
puddles, and yet—my father
is the kind of man, like God,
who would give me to the world
damaged and open,
perforated as a page, flapping
in the wind. When I stop
shaking, when you let me
sit next to the fire, next
to you, you'll want
to ask me how. I'll only tell
you the word rupture; my skin
is this blank page I fill
with batting, wound
after wound
after wound.

 ROBIN SCOFIELD

CANTALILY IMAGINES THE CREATION

She starts from a field of flowers, stars on stems.
She whittles down the daisy from original darkness.
With white light, She began the inflationary period
and it was like bread rising on instant yeast
and it gave rise to the jitters and bumps that are quasars
that spread out like so many basketballs
and it gave rise to the young stars that burned out
and left the chemicals of life, carbon and oxygen,
to mix it up with hydrogen, not aloof helium,
while She spins out the galaxies from super-novae,
those glitter bombs exploding in the heavens.
The Milky Way, open like a book before Her,
Andromeda, a small whirlpool in Her eyesight.
Cantalily looks for our little cosmos on the body
of the great Goddess, and she finds it on the left
toenail of the smallest toe, the blue and green
Earth, and all our busy ant hills, in a haze of smoke.

BRENT CANLE

MOBILE OF SEVERED LIMBS
-for, and after, Alexander Calder

Hanging from the departure center ceiling at the international airport, there is a mobile of arms—shoulders and biceps, forearms and hands—hundreds of them, thousands of them, all tied together. It must have taken years of patient persistence to obtain such perfect balance with these cauterized limbs ripped from the bodies of the living.

There's a story behind the art. The idea was first originated in the 1920s by the artist Axehandle Colander, who got his name late in his childhood when, chopping wood with laborious and heavy swings, the iron head of the axe flew into the air, severing his left and, somehow, right arms. They say the axe head caught the wind just right and boomeranged around to get him twice, cleaving each arm off from the shoulder.

Some blamed it on plain dumb luck, all the confluent forces somehow converging against the boy. Others blamed the mother, a woman of depressed lethargy who showed little to no love for her child and would only come down from her room if there was a raucous fire ablaze in the living room fireplace, one so large it put out a violent heat that threatened eyebrows and the ice cubes in the ice box. The more practical ones in town, however, blamed the wood, that apparently wasn't fond of getting chopped, though, even still, this seems like an unwarranted reaction. Whoever was to blame for the initial incident, it was absolutely the father who decided to rewedge that axe and afix it to his boy's arm. He left the left socket empty, but the right was now this axe, about a long as the boy was tall. He dragged it behind him for several years. The boy did grow into the axe eventually. Got pretty good at using it too. He got the name Axehandle for obvious reasons, but, Colander isn't his real last name. He got the name Colander because of the colander he took to wearing on his head. Started a religion too about some food aliens or something of the like, I don't know.

The point is Colander kept his dismembered arms. He played with them. He tied them together with a string and carried them around and tossed them in his teeth like nunchucks. One day, he slung them over the bough of a tree when he was chopping wood. It was a particularly oppressive day that day. And as he was wiping the sweat off his brow with the sweatband on his axe handle, he saw those little arms, his little arms, in perfect balance, swaying ever so slightly in the faintest and hottest breeze. And it was then that an artist as born.

Colander saw a vision of god that day, and god was a gigantic mobile of severed limbs. Hundred of them, balanced and dancing around one another in synchronous purpose.

But limbs, Colander came to find out, aren't all that easy to aquire. At first, he chopped them off of people who were walking to their car alone, late at night after a grueling and mind-numbing shift at some padded post-college white collar job. Then he started stalking the field of corn, jumping up on a tractor and hacking off a farm hand's arm when they weren't looking. Sometimes, it was in alleyways or bar room bathrooms. Other times, it was at an animal kill shelter, or birthday clown conferences in Fresno, or the infirmary tent at a Civil War reenactment. Eventually, he got so good at taking people's arms, Colander could be in a dense crowd and as some unsuspecting person yawned, stretching both arms up, he would snatch them right out of the air.

Now, no one knows how he put this mobile together. The level of dexterity needed to assemble such a delicate piece seems about impossible for a man with no arms, save an axe. I assume he used his teeth and feet, seems like there is little other option. However it happened, late in his life Colander revealed to the world his vision and it was, they say, revolutionary.

I don't know much about art. The whole deal seems like, to me, a thing of privilege that few people in this world are allowed the time or the energy to practice. I suppose this is why so many artist are perceived as outsiders and lunatics, who else could forgo society and family and love to such a polarity. Artists always seem to preach the boundlessness of love yet I don't see too many of them practicing it. Neither here nor there, I suppose. But what I can tell you is that I know Colander's work in a way that most will never. Can never. I'm the janitor here at the airport, I'm the only one on the graveyard shift, and once a month I have to get the scissor lift and clean this "revolutionary" piece of art. And there is something the guide books don't tell you, something that only I know: the limbs remember.

Like how people can feel phantoms limbs after so many years without it, so too can those limbs feel their phantom lives. As they hang up there they remember. You wouldn't know it from the floor of the airport but when you get up close and personal, you can see them in action. Some are typing away at absent keyboards. Other are steering the wheels of vehicles. Pulling the levers and pushing the buttons at factories. Some are sowing clothes. Others throw up gang signs. A couple seems like they are conducting orchestras or waving planes on on the tarmac. A whole bunch of them want to shake hands whenever I get close. Some pat me on the back, or rub my shoulders, or examine my teeth, or grab at my breast. Hell, there are three limbs up there that, whenever I come around, unbutton my pants, and yeah, I've let them do their thing, it gets lonely, get off your high horse, besides, not the point.

The point is most limbs are generally easy to tell what use to do, or what they are doing, or what they are trying to do. But there are some that I don't know what to make of.

I love them the most. The arms and hands which move in ways that I've never seen before.

There are a few boy arms up there. I'd like to think that one, or two, of them are Colander's but I can never know for sure. Not one of them is making the motion of swinging an axe. But then, maybe, swinging that axe wasn't what defined Axehandle Colander.

 ROBERT COLE

TWO POEMS

INQUIRY

The hermits lead through juniper ruins to find a place to rest.
Their canes assuage the wild corners and cause bleak things to rise.
We follow a fence into the trees beneath a moon we understand.

Here is a black pond, choked by algae, enclosed by trees forever.
Beneath we know a mahogany box is wrapped in dead kelp,
anchored to this root with silver wire, left to swell and be forgot.

There is no hollow built by man that contains the dark necessary.

Horatio receives the spear and beholds the oil with both hands.
Life should be sated with life. The thin momentum of ancestors.
The wind that pulls various pollinations across the fathom.

The box is retrieved from murk and wallow. The women arrive.
There must be precision now and careful eyes set to non.
It would be alright to possess a collective, singular self.

PROCESSION

We wrap his body in cheesecloth and flora.
We place a coin upon his head.

Marcus shaves poles for the pyre, inscribes a name
with the year of this gift. We sway and moan

until the platform floats. Lichen is eaten,
drink is coaxed from the barber's bandwagon.

We must rescind the doubt, haggle our lovers,
Bequeath our piss to the dangerous night.

We set the pyre ablaze, ignite our torches one by one.
Somehow our gowns are clean, white and no longer wet.

We cast our fire like sepulchers before us.
The mountain will respect our acceptance of its murder.

We each wear a mask depicting a creature our people have eaten this year.
        Solemn into the grün nochmals, immaculate mit Tieren so viele.

The women thrum inside their throats
and the children dance behind them.

PATTIE PALMER-BAKER

TWO POEMS

DEATH TAKES MY MOTHER

On the strands of a spider web
the sun plucks
an overture of light.
The sky's blue vibrates
and a nearby rose sings
a lipstick-red aria –

the color my mother wore,
although when dying,
her unpainted mouth radiated
pink that I kissed over and over
whispering wake up wake up
please wake up.

Center-stilled
in a light-storm of symmetry,
a spider waits for a passerby
who, blinded by the threads' flash,
will dive headfirst into the sink
of those sinuous strands.

My mother sways and stumbles
into the web's silken stick –
no fight, not even a token scuffle,
as the spider, jaws agape,
scuttle-stops,

scuttle-stops
nearer and nearer.
I shut my eyes, lay my face
against the rose of her cheeks –
so close to her soul
his fangs graze my heart.

THE HEREAFTER

I am nearing the dark.
Gathered in tight murders,
crows watch
and bow
to the ink-stained cloud
closing in on me.

The sun casts a sidelong glance
then drops
to the other side of the world,
too bored
with the dark
too bored
with me
to watch the gloom advancing.

As the coal-dark shadow approaches
nearby stars
watch
pulse,
and scatter glitter
coating my body in star-shed.

An angel spies my gleaming body –
not a sculpted angel
waving creamy wings.
an angel darker
than a black hole
folds me
into his stormy plumage,

flies me
to the star of his choice,
and flings me
into a flare erupting from the corona.

Beside me my mother flames.

# Joy Kennedy-O'Neill

UNDER

Emma stands at the sink, scraping a plate. The summer day is bright, and children ride bicycles around our cul-de-sac.

"Joe Nedford's going to build a pool," she says.

"Mmmm."

"Behind his house."

I put down my book. "What? But the tunnel–"

"I know. You should tell him to stop."

Joe's is the last house on our street. If he filled in his tunnel, it wouldn't ruin the whole network. But why would he and his wife do it?

I stand with Emma at the sink where I know the sound carries down through the pipes. Down to any listeners below.

"Sets a bad precedent, don't you think?" I say.

#

Our neighborhood's Green-Grove. The founders were optimists. Trees haven't grown back since the fall-out, but we've planted saplings. We have cul-de-sacs and kids on bikes now. Solar power.

The tunnels were built during the acid rain times. My grandmother lived in them. She said close-living with a whole town, down in the dark, was hard. Not just the lack of luxuries. The intimacy.

It wasn't scurvy that nearly killed them, but the coming to blows.

"Better to know things from a safe distance," she'd said.

The town still uses the tunnels, but in private. The main entrance is a trapdoor in the park's white-washed gazebo, although there's another behind the library. The passageways fan out under every street and house. Of course, the tunnels don't open into the houses. That would be rude.

Below, the dirt smells lovely. Like old books. Damp and thick. You can look up and see copper pipes and hear the mundane life above: dishes rattling, feet thudding, love-making, arguments. All the voices of daily life.

Above, the town is bright and thin-smiled. "Fine, and how are YOU?"

Below is the real nitty-gritty.

#

Emma leaves for her music club. I have no idea what I can say to Joe about his pool, so I walk the tunnels.

Neighbors don't look at each other down here in the network, where we listen. We don't speak when we pass, pressing against the cool dirt walls. Oil lanterns hiss and sputter. They're strings of amber pearls.

Under #45 Wood-dale I hear the Smith's girl. "I'm looking in the mirror and I'm in my best dress and I'm pretty!"

Hmm. Such a selfer-shout, but most of the kids do it. Tomorrow I'll stand in my kitchen and speak loudly "That Smith girl seems to be getting vain."

It will all come back to the right person on its own.

I hear coughing and sneezing from #47. Either Bill or Margo have a cold. I'll ask Emma to make them a casserole.

From below #22 Oak, I can hear strains of Mozart and my wife's voice rising.

"He never does a thing I ask. Not a thing! He sits there reading books and doesn't say a word about the dinner or compliments me. Just a big fat lug."

My gut twists. Knowing what people really think about you – well. Truth is dirt-dark, but there's a beauty in it. It's worm-truth. People's mouths open like caves.

#

"You didn't speak to Joe?" Emma asks.

"No. But I'll go." I put down my book. "By the way, dinner was wonderful last night. I forgot to tell you."

"Thank you."

I walk down the sidewalk to where other neighbors watch the construction at Joe's. The workers have already poured the concrete, filling in his tunnel.

We men shift our feet and clear our throats.

"That's something."

None of us knock on his door.

#

Below, I look at the new blockage. Joe's house is silent now. He's off the grid. Why? I've heard him and his wife making love. Their marriage seems to be fine.

#

"We'll go together," Emma says. She makes cookies and puts on a nice pair of heels.

Joe greets us warmly when we knock. "Come in!"

"Oh no," Emma smiles. "We just heard about your pool."

"Yes! We'll have the whole neighborhood over. Like an old-fashioned social."

"That'll be nice."

We endure a silence.

Joe's wife tries to give Emma a hug, but Emma thrusts the cookies into her hands.

Joe pats my shoulder. "Come over for pool parties! We'll talk. Share stuff. You know, in person."

"Thank you," I shake his hand stiffly.

But I know I won't come over again. No one will. Who would want to hear their truths up top, spinning in the sunlight, sharp and harsh as blue chlorine?

Emma and I walk back in silence, defeated, with just the clicking staccato of her heels.

I want to tell her she's beautiful in the falling summer light, but it will seem insincere coming firsthand.

I'm surprised when she wipes away a tear.

"They've gone mad," she says. "Absolutely mad!"

End

Small Snaked

CHRIS BULLARD

ART

The itinerant silhouette artist comes to your house to do portraits. He puts his hands on your brother's shoulders and turns him sideways. Directing a spotlight on your brother's figure, he creates an outline on the wall. With a hammer and a chisel he chips away at the plaster to create a cavity that's in the exact shape of the shadow. "Bravo," your father shouts. Your mother claps. After he positions your brother inside the hole, he carves out two spaces for your father and mother. They take their places in a tableau and he seals each niche with tar. "Beautiful," your father declares from inside the wall. Your mother exclaims, "You've caught our likenesses perfectly." "I really feel like I'm part of the family," your brother says. "How about me?" you ask the silhouette artist. He grips your hand and pulls you outside where he directs you to lie on the lawn. He uses a brush with white paint to draw around your body. When you stand up, he gives you a shovel. You begin digging a grave in your own shape. You're learning to be an artist.

 Lynn Pattison

DREAM

house of folded paper
         blood smudged from edge-cut fingers

sand streams up in the blue-tinted hourglass

a lifetime of unopened letters
         nailed to the willow stump

violet gases from fallow garden beds
         like Hermes scarves winding
               the Queen's neck

seven women in red leotards—
            each with an onyx box

the letters signify toil,
         red garb: penalty

but it's cobwebs
      sagging the humid morning
            that scare her awake

 KRISTEN HAVENS

DO, DO, DO

Catherine stood in the corner of the tea shop, staring the spider down.

Simply dreadful, whispered Lady Jane. *Doesn't it make you shiver to look at it?*

She shook her head. The spider was the size of her daddy's thumb. Gray and fuzzy, it clung to the underside of a dusty display table. Looming above were candles—heavy ones that could tip and fall, flattening a five-year-old like a pancake.

"So don't touch anything," her mother had warned, before wandering off.

She means bugs too, you know.

Unh-unh, said Catherine. Lady Jane was a 'fraidy cat, always worrying about touching the wrong things or getting caught. But Catherine's mother was on the far side of the shop now, looking at tea tins. Dumb brother Brendan lay beside her in his stroller. Nobody was watching. What was the harm in trying to pet one spider?

It'll bite you.

Catherine didn't think so. Not if she took it fast. Still, it couldn't hurt to check first. She seized Lady Jane's hand and yanked it toward the furry body. Lady Jane cried out and pulled free.

Ow! Don't be rude!

All right, foo-foo. Whiner. *I* will get the spider.

I'll tell. They'll send you away to that place.

Catherine struggled not to pinch her. Lady Jane always chose times like this to visit. Times when fascinating things might happen. She fretted and worried and made Catherine's head hurt with her rules. *Do, do, do play with that doll. Do, do, do lower your dress, they can see between your legs. Smile. Say your prayers. Play nice.*

Lady Jane lived far away. When she visited it was rude to tell her to go. Catherine knew all about rude. Her father was rude, slamming down the phone when strangers called. When her mother said "rude," her hand struck fast like a snake before sinking beneath the couch cushions.

Catherine did not want to be rude. Though Lady Jane touched all her best toys and told her, in her own house, what she could and could not do, she abided her. Most days she waited for her visitor to grow bored and leave.

Not today, Lady Jane said. *I know what you're planning.*

The spider kept its tiny red eyes on them.

Catherine inched forward, holding her skirt still.

I will tell, Catherine. I will tell her what's in your pocket.

But there were other rules too. Rules made by children.

Catherine closed her eyes and pictured Lady Jane's house of gingerbread. The stale roof, the sticky floor, the throne coated in molasses. This was where Lady Jane sat when she wasn't needed. Stuck like a piece of unwrapped candy at the bottom of a diaper bag. Like a fly in a web. Like a dollhouse doll at the bottom of a skirt pocket.

Bye bye, friend.

When Catherine opened her eyes, Lady Jane had vanished.

She leaned forward with both hands open to take the spider and make it her own.

RYAN SCARIANO

TWO POEMS

WHAT I THOUGHT IN THE MOMENT BEFORE MY DEATH

Praise to the insects blooming for the machine.
And praise to the red alders along the road, still leafless,
smoldering so mossy green. So green, I picked the lock
on the hummingbird's heart only to find
another dirty machine burning oil. But it's okay
because the croaking frogs splatter fat new raindrops
and spring's old song plays loud on the radio.
Like a poor kid dribbling his basketball
through tired streets, I think I know
the broken stone's desire to crumble.
I'm a dead man digging my grave with a deer bone.
My grave in the dawn and the careful noise
from the port wafting out over the sound.

MARMOT ROAD

Trying to get to Nate's place,
I turned on Marmot Road
when I should've stayed
on Ten Eyck to Bull Run.
I wound through the forest
broken by wet pasture and Holsteins,
past a barn leaning against
a hand-lettered sign for eggs.
Though I knew I was lost, I hummed
along the Devil's Backbone
with the big river on one side
and the little river on the other.
My ears popped. The moss
and lichen flashed like sunshine
in my eyes. Was I driving toward
the original marmot, still
dreaming in his burrow
by a secret clear lake?
But there never have been
marmots in these parts.
Night fell and I broke down
by the muddy roadside creek.
Yet, as the moon clouded,
this sad trickle off the mountain
eased through a culvert and pooled
in a brownish-black puddle
amid cedar and hemlock.
My dark earth was ripe with
the fertile scents.

Here the primordial mountain beaver
found me. Unexpectedly,
I prayed to her for ten million years
as she counted her stars
and ate fiddleheads.

Matthew Chamberlin

CAME IN MAY

Came in May's lewd dandelion days
a parcel, bent and frowning,
browning in the porch-hot noon
and labeled simply *Them.*

It sat unopened in the parlor. Some weeks on
the thing began to pulse within,
all brown and rent the paper burst.
Soon filled the room with scrapling shreds
who cried and spoke, small gallop-folk
of budding parchment spark and bloom
who chased with rarest wanton bounds
among the chairs about the room
then stopped, chagrined,
to blossom into flame and flowers.

I, idle in my curiosities, discovered I one pallid noon
whilst masticating mouth-bud bulbs
myself, and all about myself
without the tattered shreds of all
had lain within the baggy box,
the foxy onion-paper bag
all flayed and rinsed, so flensed of spirit,
minced with bitten teeth and sharp

that seemed to me in code of mottle-stain
to say to me in drip-drip code
of morsel-tap, *come in.*

Within I found a bit of seashore blue,
a paper folded blue
and pink
which when I teased it open,

flung the winds of all my hate
upon the shred of it,
laid all my winds upon the door
the boards the floor of it,
and threw my words of greed and rue
upon the grain of it,
flew open,

and gave in

C.J. SPATARO

TONY THE TIGER

Her husband, Rob, stands in their California living room. The sun streams through the French doors that lead to the pool out back. The sunlight frames Rob's body like a halo. Penny assumes that's what he's hoping. He never misses an opportunity to set up a shot and get it just right. Rob is trying to convince her that she should put on a Tony the Tiger costume and travel back in time. He wants to play a prank on Aretha Franklin. He thinks this is hilarious. Penny doesn't know why Rob thinks time travel is so funny, but he does. Every once in a while he gets it in his head to send her back in time to play a trick on one of his friends. He's staring at her with his *I can talk you into anything* face. Penny crosses her arms and frowns. She hates that face.

"Why 1979? Why can't we just go to her house now?" She unfolds her arms and leans forward. "I don't want to put on that big furry head and shout, 'That's grrreat!'"

He sits down and pulls Penny to him. "I want to make some new memories," he says. He folds her under his bear arm.

"If we go visit her today, tomorrow it will be a memory," she says.

He nuzzles her ear. His beard is rough against her cheek. Even after all these years, this tactic frequently works on her and she sighs, disgusted with herself. "It's not the same," he says. "You know how this works."

She pulls away, and slides down the sleek mid-century couch. "It's almost fifty years. What makes you think you'll remember it anyway?"

"Penny, come on. You know I'll remember. I always remember."

She does know. Rob has hyperthymesia, which she finds incredibly annoying at times like this. Actually, she finds it annoying almost all of the time. He can't forget anything, even if he wanted to. And because of his hyperthymesia he periodically is able to convince Penny to go back in time and create a new memory for him. He doesn't have to do anything. Penny is the one taking all the risks, doing all the work. For a guy who's considered a comedy genius, it's always the same joke, too. She's wearing some kind of outlandish costume, shows up at someone's house while he's there visiting, and says something completely out of context. She knows it's her voice that cracks him up. That, and the costume. She supposes she should be grateful that after all these years he still finds her voice amusing.

"You're the only one I trust," he says smiling.

"What if something goes wrong?" she says, regretting it as soon as it comes out of her mouth.

"Nothing can go wrong." He's working up a head of steam. His eyes narrow, he's puffing out his lips. "Scientists have proven that time is an—"

"—immutable stream," she says, finishing his speech. He glares at her and she looks at her lap.

"We can't go back and kill Hitler, or Stalin, or Genghis Khan, no matter how much we want to. Scientists have tried. What's meant to happen, happens." He looks at her and takes a deep breath. He's trying not to shout. They've been married long enough for her to know that he's trying to calm down. He doesn't want to be a bully. He just really wants what he wants. "What we can do," he says smiling again, "is pull some stellar practical jokes on people."

Penny exhales. "But what if I set off some tiny paradox that causes the two of us to never meet?" She looks out the window at the light glinting off their shimmering pool. "We've been lucky so far, although right now," she pauses, "not meeting you doesn't seem all bad." She gives him a half smile to let him know that she's not entirely serious.

"The chances of changing anything significant are very low—you know that. This is why time travel is available, because there are so few risks." He runs his hand over his bald head, something he does when he's irritated. "Time is a closed loop. We can't change anything important that hasn't already happened."

"But there have been cases where little things have changed. I can't go back and assassinate anyone or change the course of politics, but I could change the course of our lives." She takes his hand. He is her husband and she hates to remind him of these things, but she feels like she doesn't have a choice. "Neither one of us is that important."

"That's where you're wrong, Penny," he says. "We've shaped the course of American comedy. We're important."

She shakes her head. On this point, they disagree. Always. She thinks that maybe if they'd had kids that would have created some kind of permanence. Penny had a daughter, from her first marriage, who died in her twenties, but she and Rob were never able have any of their own. Maybe if they had, he would think differently about risking it all for a joke. Penny misses her daughter every day. If she could go back in time and tell her not to get in the car, to take a different route, she would. She's tried more than once, but her daughter always dies some different way. Or she dies the same way on a different day. It's too much and Penny has stopped trying.

She shakes her head, focuses on the task at hand. "Rob, we're not Marie Curie and Albert Einstein. We're just a couple of schlubs from New York, living the high life, lucky enough that people think we're funny."

"Come on, Pen," Rob says. He juts out his lower lip in an exaggerated pout.

She does not want to travel back in time, but she will. She always does what Rob wants.

Time travel is not so tough from a physical standpoint. It's kind of like riding a Tilt-a-Whirl. Penny likes amusement rides, so the dizzy, spinning feeling doesn't bother her so much. Scientists, historians, and idiots with too much money are really the only people who indulge in time travel any more. This is Penny's tenth trip. She is worried that she'll change something that will matter only to her and that only she'll remember, because she's the traveler. She thinks that's the real reason why Rob won't play these jokes himself. He doesn't want to be the one to remember how things used to be. With his hyperthymesia the paradox could make him crazy. Maybe.

Penny's read stories online about how travelers come back to their present and have two different versions of the past stuck in their heads. Most learn to live with a dual past, but some don't. The fact that Rob is willing to risk their relationship, and her sanity, makes her mad enough to do it. December 1979 was a rocky time for them. They were teetering close to divorce. Penny's not so excited about heading back to that time and visiting that Rob.

The plan is for Penny to teleport to Aretha Franklin's Encino, California home, ring the doorbell and shout, "That's grrreat!" Then she'll remove her tiger head, tell them she's from the future, and teleport back home. Rob will fill her in on Aretha's hilarious (he hopes) reaction when she returns. Penny wonders why Rob really was at Aretha's. He says he was there to try to convince her to guest on *All in the Family*. The ratings were sliding by then—everyone could see the end coming, but Penny suspects there were other reasons.

She zips up the tiger suit. Rob thinks with Aretha's Michigan roots she'll get a kick out of the Tony the Tiger outfit. Penny doesn't get it at first, but Rob explains: Detroit Tigers, Kellogg's is in Battle Creek, Michigan. She shrugs, unconvinced. Before Penny puts on the head, he leans in and kisses her on the cheek. Penny is in her early 70s. She can't help but acknowledge the absurdity of the situation. Part of her thinks it is pretty funny, her standing there in a Tony the Tiger suit, but another part of her is thinking it is ridiculous, and not in a good way. She fixes Rob with her gaze.

"What?" he says.

"I'm too old for this shit," she says. She pulls on the head while Rob dials up the time and place on the wormhole generator. She lifts the head up slightly, so he can understand her. "This is the last time I'm going to do this, just so you know."

Rob looks at her with a sad expression on his face. "It probably is," he says.

"I love you," she says through the mask.

The wormhole is swirling in the middle of the living room and Rob taps his ear like he can't hear. He's so full of it, Penny thinks.

She rolls her eyes in the safety of her furry head and steps through the wormhole. There's the expected vertigo and then Aretha Franklin's Encino door. She rings the bell and when the burly butler answers, she hands him a note that says: *I'm from the Acme singing telegram company. Rob Reiner sent me.* He laughs and waves her in. "Wait here," he says. He leaves and returns quickly. "Follow me," he says and leads Penny up a grand curving staircase to Aretha's master bedroom. The room is opulent, white shag carpet on the floor and a mink throw on the king-sized bed. Aretha is wearing a cobalt peignoir and Rob, in all his 70s Meathead glory, is lying on the bed wearing a paisley silk kimono tied at his waist. "What the fuck?" Penny roars inside the Tony the Tiger head.

Aretha, who had been smiling, stands with her hands on her hips. "Who the hell are you?" she says.

Penny removes the tiger head and shakes out her hair. Rob looks like he's going to throw up, but Aretha just looks confused. "I was supposed to say, 'That's grrreat!' but under the circumstances, I'm not sure I can do that," Penny says. She holds the tiger head under her arm like a helmet. They stare at her, mouths agape. If Rob wanted a memory, Penny is going to oblige him. He had to have remembered what he had been doing here. He hadn't been there convincing Aretha of anything, except maybe they had time for one more quickie. He must have wanted Penny to see this for some reason.

"I'm from the future," she says. "Rob thought this would be funny." She looks at the young Rob who's pulled his legs together and has tightened the belt on his robe. "Why is this funny? I mean, I'm an old woman now, and you, I'm starting to think, are still an asshole."

Rob is unable to speak. He looks at Penny mutely and gives her an open-palmed shrug. Aretha turns her gaze to Penny and shakes her head as only the queen of soul can.

She purses her lips as she stares hard at Rob. "You are an asshole," she says to him.

He gets up off the bed and comes toward Penny. She remembers that face, how he used to look at her. He still has most of his hair, his eyes are bright, and that mustache—it's too much. He grasps her by the shoulders and looks down into her face. "You're so old," he says.

"No shit, genius," Penny says. "That's what happens in the future."

"How old are you?"

She rolls her eyes and sighs. "We'll talk about this when I get home. You've got some explaining to do." She pokes him in the chest and he backs up.

"Time travel?" Aretha says.

"Since 2002," Penny says. "Most people don't bother, since time is a closed loop. Supposedly, you can't change anything that matters."

"Is that so?" Aretha says.

"Scientists and idiots say so," Penny says.

Aretha looks at Rob. "Why was I supposed to think this was funny?"

Rob shrugs. "I have no idea. Maybe I have dementia?"

"I know that for me, this whole thing is forty some years in the past." Penny pauses to gesture with her paw between Rob and Aretha. "But finding out that your husband is, or was, sleeping with another woman is a little disconcerting."

"I'm sorry you had to find out this way, honey," Aretha says.

Penny sets the tiger head on the end of the bed. She looks at Rob, at how he doesn't even seem to feel sorry. "Can I use your phone?" she asks Aretha.

Aretha nods toward the purple slim line next to the bed.

"What's our number, Rob?"

"You don't remember our number?"

"I'm from the future. Do you remember every phone number you've ever had?"

He leans back against the footboard of the bed. "Well—"

Penny stops him with a wave of her paw. Of course he remembers every phone number, stupid, fucking hyperthymesia. He shoves his hands in his kimono pockets and tells her the number. She punches it out with furry fingers and waits for the answering machine to beep, and then she leaves herself a long message. She sets the phone back in its cradle. It's so weird to see a phone with a cord, she thinks. Aretha has turned away from both of them. She's sitting at her vanity powdering her neck. Penny doesn't know what to do either.

"It was nice to meet you, Miss Franklin," Penny says. "I wish it had been under different circumstances." She looks up at Penny in the mirror then turns to face her. They're both so young, Penny's a little unnerved.

"Can you tell me what's going to happen?"

"I could," Penny says. She reaches for her tiger head. "But it won't make any difference."

"I guess I'll just have to be surprised then," she says.

Penny looks at Rob. "Surprises suck."

When she arrives back in her own time, Penny does not teleport back into her living room. The nausea and dizziness is almost overwhelming when she steps through the portal. She's never felt this sick before. She looks around the room and it is new and familiar at the same time. The rug is oriental and the furniture is not the sleek mid-century she's expecting but instead is transitional. The colors are deep and warm. She remembers picking out the rug with her daughter two years ago at a swap meet and she swoons slightly. There are no French doors, no pool just beyond the great room, no Rob. She lurches forward, trembling. She's afraid she's going to vomit inside the tiger mask and she steadies herself by grabbing the arm of the couch. She sits and removes the tiger head and throws it across the room. It skitters across the hardwood floor and slides to a stop face up, staring back at her. On the mantle, there are photos of her daughter with her husband taken at her daughter's thirtieth birthday party. There are photos of her grandchildren. She recognizes them all and she doesn't. Tears spring to her eyes and she feels as if her head might crack open.

Is this what Rob wanted? She sighs. This is what he wanted. He didn't want a divorce, he wanted a different life. It hits her all at once like two swirling strands of a braid, two flowing channels of memories—one with Rob and one without. She sits on the couch and breathes deeply trying to steady the nausea. Eventually, the room starts to quiet and her breathing slows and she doesn't feel quite so sick. She's so angry she wants to call Rob, but it won't do any good. He won't remember their life together, only their life apart. That's what he wanted all along. His life without her. Now she's stuck with these two divergent timelines in her head. She looks up and sees the photo of her daughter, closes her eyes, and focuses on her two grandsons. She remembers a life with and without them too: their births, changing their diapers, their first days of school. She is overcome with the sounds and the smells of them. She's so happy her chest feels as if it's constricting and expanding at the same time. She blinks hard, not sure who she should call first.

Michael Brosnan

NEGATIVE NUMBERS

Try explaining this to a child:
We can't touch them, only draw them as stick figures.

And yet they tug all day, spirit-like, as pointless
as the constant nagwish to live betterlives.

How does it feel being opposite of obvious,
being something we can know but never embrace?

They are not the milky moon to the singeing sun.
Nor the erasure of time to time imagined.

They are more a fractured memory
that stays stubbornly young in the mind as you age,

as you wander and wonder and worry and ache.
They wait silently in shadows of places

we forget to return to.
No one comes by to explain why.

ROB ENGLE

ON OFF ON

somewhere in the fourth dimension   your body is
a prism   every wound an entrance for light your
teeth   nodes of a prayer   a face is a stream
of binary code   it's easier to make out   in analog
form   with signals of information   passed by
a continuously variable physical quantity   like
telling how much a doorway is open   or not or
charting your skin's history   start by spreading
yourself   out across the table   like a map
reference the legend   of your navel   one inch to
a trauma   the span of your shoulders   inversely
proportional   to the amount of room left   inside
your home   after a dinner party   when the dishes
are   stacked but not washed   you are full
but not finished

LILY IONA MACKENZIE

OUT TO SEA

10th Day

The ship's captain and her first mate expect too much from me, the only other person on this ship. Since coming aboard, I've worked constantly—sweeping, scrubbing, polishing wood and brass, preparing meals. Not the way I usually spend my days.

The women made it clear the first days were crucial: we needed to do extra duty in order to reach a destination the captain was pushing for by the tenth day. So this is the tenth day and where are we? And why would I so readily follow their orders?

If they had found me during the day, I may have resisted or at least taken time to consider and question. But I was sound asleep when the foghorn howled from the pier near my house and drew me to it. I've always been intrigued by the sea, and foghorns seem so romantic, Poseidon's voice coming from the depths. Both plaintiff and insistent, it floated over the water and land like a specter.

I couldn't refuse.

Half asleep, I stumbled across my brick walkway leading to the water's edge. At first I thought the ghostly-looking ship was lost in the fog, needing directions. But the women in charge of it seemed to know exactly where they were and what they were after. If anyone were lost, it appeared to be me.

They didn't waste any time with niceties. Their instructions were terse and clipped, floating over the water. We're lowering a rowboat. Get into it. Row till you reach the ship. Climb the ladder onto the deck. We sail before dawn.

The vessel resembled ones I've seen in pirate movies from another era, its sails flapping in the wind, the masts pointing at the sky. It appealed to all my dreamy notions of sailing around the world and visiting exotic ports.

But I need to pack a bag, I protested, my sleep-dazed mind still practical.

We have everything you need.

In that moment, I couldn't imagine disobeying those commanding, regal women. Once on board, the black night enclosed us, and the fog shut out the rest of the world. Even the moon was hidden.

The next day I learned I was to keep the ship's log. They want some kind of record to leave behind. Why, I don't know. They didn't give me any instructions, so I'm writing what seems important to me. This is the first day I've had time to do it.

Whenever I have a free moment (and those aren't many), I study the women standing their watch at the ship's wheel. Both seem slightly familiar to me. Faces impenetrable, they could be sisters.

Speaking of sisters, I feel a little like Cinderella, and they remind me of the wicked stepsisters. Both have long hair the color of the ocean's depths, their skin white as foam. Their fine clothes—flowing caftans, a piercing purple color with gold trim around the neck—don't resemble my rough rags: I'm wearing an ugly ankle-length muslin dress, the color of wheat. It scratches my skin and resembles a sack. Straight lines conceal my curves, but there's no man to look at them anyway. They gave me the dress to replace the nightgown I wore when I boarded the ship.

If there weren't something so otherworldly about the two, they would be beautiful. But it's a cold beauty, to be gazed at, not to be touched. I shiver just looking at them, and a low-grade anxiety gnaws at my stomach whenever they're near.

Sometimes the fog lifts enough to reveal the cold and menacing sea. Waves beat against the ship's worn boards, the ocean a prehistoric beast awakened from a long sleep.

When I'm on deck, the fog strokes my face and hands and moistens my skin. But I'm hungry for warmth, for the sun's dry, penetrating heat. I'm also lost without a painting to work on or any oil paints to play with. My palette feels like an extension of my arm. Being without it must be similar to what a mother feels when she's separated from her young child for a period of time. I have an ache inside, an empty space that the artworks fill.

A sail snaps in the wind and the rigging creaks from the sudden gust that fills the mainsail. Sea gulls screech overhead, hoping to snatch scraps of food. I throw them the rest of my meager meal of freeze dried fruits and vegetables. A few grains of rice. They attack the scraps and gulp them down. I stare at them, picturing what they might be like plucked and roasted on a spit. My mouth waters in anticipation.

11th Day

Okay, no great surprise: I'm wondering again why I'm here. I've had no time to ask questions, but my captors haven't encouraged communication. Why did I leave my comfortable beach cottage? The mural I'm working on? My friends? Stephen? What is this journey's purpose?

12th Day

Progress. I've learned one woman's name. A sudden gust of wind slammed into the mainsail and pushed us off course, causing the first mate to call out "Circe, Circe" to the captain, who was studying a map.

The one called Circe grabbed the wheel, a wild look in her eyes, as if she were challenging the sea...the wind. The ship keeled and waves washed over the sides, but Circe whipped us about so the wind was no longer caught in the sail. Soon we had righted ourselves and were moving forward. She glanced triumphantly at her first mate.

Circe isn't a name you hear every day. Or even every other day. Still, she's famous. Everyone knows about Circe the sorceress who seduced Odysseus and changed his men into pigs. I think he managed to escape her sorcery with Hermes' help. Complicated tale. Complicated woman.

I wouldn't mind having that kind of power. It isn't that I want to turn men into animals. I like the opposite sex. I want to keep them around. But I like to transform other things, bring beauty where there isn't any. The murals I make are an attempt to titivate institutions—banks, schools, offices. It's my way of infiltrating an otherwise drab corporate world and bringing some life to it. Stimulating the imagination.

Georgia O'Keefe inspired me with the big flowers she painted, her way of making viewers see things we take for granted and usually don't notice. I try to do something similar and have been thinking of how to enliven this ship with images. Something nautical. Sea life. Moon jellies. Urchins. Sea horses. Magical creatures. But with no tools, I have to rely on envisioning these things, not capturing them in acrylics or oils.

The other woman seems like Circe's shadow. She gives me a list each day of chores that must be done: cooking, cleaning, scrubbing the deck, keeping watch—a responsibility they only recently entrusted me with, but I haven't a clue what I'm watching for. If they only knew what a poor sense of direction I have. It's a wonder I didn't get lost just leaving my mother's womb.

Today we ate together for the first time. It wasn't exactly fine dining. No one spoke. We avoided each other's eyes. Or I should say, they avoided my attempts to make eye contact. I was filled with questions, but they give off a strange vibe. Maybe we couldn't converse even if we tried. We might speak the same language, but are we in the same universe? Yet they talk to one another, and sometimes I overhear bits and pieces of words that pass between them like a tight rope: water, waves, food, sleep, sky. Not abstractions... not ideas.

I'm dreaming more intensely than I ever have before. I awaken in the night, unable to distinguish at times between my dreams and life aboard this ship, which seems more and more like a dream.

13th Day

I'm making some progress. I learned the other woman's name today. While Circe was at the wheel, her first mate came below for some hot broth. I was at the stove when she entered. As I handed her the cup of steaming soup, our eyes met for the first time. I felt a shock of recognition. I know this woman.

Words rose to my lips, and I found myself saying, Here's your soup, Tarista. Her sea-green eyes widened. The boat rocked. But she didn't ask me how I knew her name. I couldn't have told her anyhow. She clutched the cup, abruptly turned away from me, and swept out of the galley.

I must have been right about the name because she didn't deny it. Later, I caught the two of them watching me closely, appearing as curious about me as I am about them. Their response is a surprise. I thought they knew everything about me. I hadn't considered they aren't as all knowing as I assumed.

14th Day

I've just written "14th Day," but I'm not experiencing time in the usual sense. There's really nothing to indicate night or day except that we sleep for a certain number of hours and then we're awake for even more time. Day and night blend into the neutralizing grey fog that clings to and encloses us. It lifts slightly now and then to hint at something beyond but immediately closets us again. Need I say it's oppressive? I used to like fog, the way it softens whatever it touches, blurs sharp edges. I try to do something similar in my paintings. But I can't think of it positively now that it won't go away.

How in hell have we travelled in dense fog? How have we managed with only three people making up the crew? I ask these questions, but I don't get any answers.

The longer I'm aboard, the more this feels like a ghost ship, propelled, directed, and assisted by some force only Circe and Tarista understand. No radar guides them in these waters; nor are there any buoys or signposts. The only other visible living creatures are sea gulls, and they follow rather than lead us.

Today at dinner I asked Circe our destination and how long it would take us to get there. She stared at me coldly, her icy glance turning my flesh into goose bumps. At first I thought she was going to ignore my question and stomp off. But after a long, uncomfortable silence she spoke, her voice slicing the air between us, sharp enough to cut a path through the fog. The destination will be revealed soon enough, she said. Just keep to your daily tasks.

15th Day

I'm homesick. Whatever elevated thoughts I've had about this being a spiritual journey have dissolved. I almost believed these powerful females sought me out to do certain tasks that would transform me in the same way as Psyche was.

I'm afraid I've been reading too much mythology. It's made me delude myself into thinking eternal life might really exist. I like to believe we can transcend our earthly limitations, this body and our limited imaginations. Art does that for me. Whenever I'm engaged in a painting, I feel transported and can imagine something similar happening after death: maybe we enter the afterlife as one does a work of art, getting lost in it. But at the moment, eternal life seems appalling, especially if it resembles these days at sea. Who needs it?

I want to go home. I want to hold my cat. I want my lover Stephen to hold *me*. I want to sleep in my bed, wear my own clothes, eat real food again.

I definitely don't want to be here.

What would happen if I went on strike, refused to work, got sick? Would they decide I wasn't worth it and return me to my home? But why go to all that trouble? They could as easily dump me overboard. Then the sharks could savor my flesh, using my bones as toothpicks.

Stephen would say, You're overreacting, you're too impatient. Of course, if he were here, he wouldn't be stuck in the cabin half the time, a galley slave. He'd be steering the boat, telling the women what to do. Maybe that's why we're attracted to each other. I'm much more retiring than he is. But how do you explain love? It's so difficult to escape once you're in its grasp.

Does he wonder where I am? Or have I entered a black hole, a time warp? If he does find me missing, will he just interpret it as an attempt to force him to leave his wife? Of course, being a minister, he has a lot of external expectations to live up to. He's just as trapped as I am, caught by others' needs for an authority figure.

And what of me? What's attracted me to him if not his power as a man of the Word? Am I any different from other women in the congregation who are drawn to this man of God?

What influence do I have over him, if any at all? I know that I give him something his wife doesn't, something he hungers for, something he can't live without. Or so he says. And it isn't just sex, though that's part of it. A big part.

Mystery, possibility, uncertainty, challenge, depth: I'm not part of the conventional world he values. I don't have a real job. I'm not dependent on the establishment for a living because of my grandmother's inheritance. I'm not a homemaker. I'm an artist and not just a dabbler, able to make fantastic things happen on blank canvases and bring into existence something new.

All of these things both frighten and attract him. My resistance to his values, to his religion, puzzles him. I've tried to be a believer. In fact, we met in his church. I was doing volunteer work, attending adult education classes, seeking answers to my many questions about religion and my own spiritual direction, but I wasn't finding them there. If anything, I felt more confused. Stephen's god had died and been resurrected, saving the human race in the process. Through Jesus, God became human and redeemed us.

But Stephen's god is a man, and I feel strange worshiping a male god. Incomplete. Actually, I feel strange worshipping any god. Any external force. Something is missing, though it's still difficult for me to articulate exactly what it is. I just know that Christianity isn't for me.

In spite of my feelings, Stephen and I were attracted instantly—or maybe because of them. The energy between us is so intense, it's hard to be in the same room. I can't concentrate when I'm around him or even when I'm alone now. All I can think about is the shape of his lips, how vulnerable and sensuous they look framed by a beard, like a woman's labia.

Stephen doesn't come across as a minister. He seems too wild, too sensual, with his unruly black curls, his mocking smile. There's nothing of the Christianized Christ in him. Nothing of the meek and mild Palestinian. No, Stephen's true god is Dionysus. He's more abandoned than controlled, more unpredictable than doctrinaire.

But he doesn't know it, and I threaten all he holds dear: his wife, his children, his church.

16th Day

Last night I couldn't sleep. I paced my tiny space. It's not much bigger than a large closet, and there isn't a porthole, so I easily feel claustrophobic. I have a bed the width of a coffin built into a wall that always feels like its sweating. There's an area next to the bed about three feet wide and six foot long. I can smell rat shit and urine, though I haven't seen one yet. I just hear scratching in the dark.

I'm realizing I may never get off this boat or away from these women. The prospect frightens me as much as getting trapped in a bad marriage.

Unable to sleep, I tried to make mental pictures, work out ideas for future murals, but my mind kept slipping away to thoughts of Stephen. I sent him telepathic messages to rescue me. He must have the police out looking for me, a missing person. But how can he explain to the cops his relationship with me? A friend? A parishioner he's concerned about?

Maybe I've always been a missing person, absent in some major way from life. Out to sea. Swimming against the tide. Unanchored.

The artist's call reached me early, in my teens. I became physically ill when I thought of living a conventional life like my mother's. My fears were translated into an appendix attack and I needed surgery to remove it. Losing my appendix paralleled giving up any notion of marrying, having kids, and conforming to social expectations. Instead, I chose Art as my spouse, and I've never been sorry that I did. A demanding lover, he has taken me more deeply into myself than any man could have.

Still, it hasn't been easy. Guilt continues to plague me. Why? At the time, it seemed unnatural, going against nature. But male artists have made that kind of commitment and not been criticized for it. Why shouldn't women dedicate themselves to something other than children and leading a predictable existence? Why should they have to do both and never succeed fully at one or the other?

Mary Cassatt and Emily Carr have been my guides into this strange marriage. They never wed, proving that a woman can flourish in all ways through her art. Reading their biographies gave me hope. I also was lucky that my grandmother encouraged my vocation and gave me the financial means to follow it. She had wanted to be a dancer, but her father forbid it. Even as an old woman it pained her talk about the loss she suffered.

As for me, the rest is history. Or herstory. Mine.

But my story is changing, and I'm not sure I like the direction it's taking. I may threaten Stephen's tidy situation, but his effect on me is much worse. He pokes holes in my armor, the first man I would put before my creative pursuits just so I could be with him permanently. That scares the hell out of me.

There. I've said it. These thoughts have been lurking in the shadows for a long time. I just never had the courage to face them before. Me give up my freedom for a man? Never, I would have said a few months ago.

Now I'm not so sure.

Stephen. Can you hear me?

17th Day

I finally got to sleep last night, though it was close to dawn when I nodded off. It seemed like just minutes later when Tarista banged on my door and demanded breakfast. This may come as a surprise to you dear reader, as I'm sure it did to my hosts, but I told her to get lost. I needed my sleep. I'm tired of their dominance and my servility.

Since I didn't see her face, I don't know what her reaction was. And I don't care. I fell into a light sleep where I seemed to be both dreaming and awake, watching myself dream. Circe and Tarista had lured Stephen onto the boat, flashing their gorgeous long legs and offering glasses of wine the color of their painted lips. Of course, their seduction tactics worked, and he followed them into their stateroom, resembling a puppy on a leash, eager to please. He was wearing the tight denims I love so much: they show off his shapely buttocks and other treasures. Not to be left out, I followed the three of them. They had started to make out and didn't seem surprised to see me, so I flung off my clothes and joined them. The four of us found lots of inventive ways to have sex, including a little bestiality. Circe showed her true talents and turned Stephen into a pig with a large erection. But I woke up before I could try it out.

This dream shows how much I'm missing this man, though I wouldn't want to share him with these women. It's bad enough that he has a wife. Maybe it also is communicating that Stephen is thinking of me. Most important, it makes me see Circe and Tarista differently. They seem more human, with desires not unlike my own.

I realize now I needn't be their servant. Why have I let them order me around? I don't even let Stephen do that. I'm amazed at myself for boarding this ship so docilely. Like a timid sheep. And all these days that I put up with their intimidation. Unbelievable!

I'm going to insist that they return me to shore, pronto. If they don't, I'll sabotage their journey in some way. I'm beyond caring about my safety. I want to be free from my imprisonment here, even if it means losing my life. What kind of existence would it be under their thumb?

18th Day

I understand better why I'm aboard this ship. These women aren't enemies. They also aren't strangers. I've always been living with them. That's why Tarista looked so familiar, as did Circe, though it took me awhile to place them. They've inhabited my dreams and my thoughts for longer than I can remember, Circe the hard-driving female who wants to dominate men, and Tarista the artist (I just noticed that the word artist is concealed in her name) who has urged me to focus on art, at times to the exclusion of other things.

Both looked startled when I burst into the pilothouse and said I recognize you and you no longer can control me. Circe stared straight ahead at the roiling ocean, both hands on the wheel; Tarista kept her eyes focused on my shoes, her face flushing.

I insisted they return me to shore immediately.

Circe let how a muffled laugh and poked her partner. Now it was *my* turn to be startled. Laughter wasn't the response I expected. Some joke, but I'm afraid it's on them.

This time I didn't return to my cubbyhole with the rats. I headed for their stateroom and made myself comfortable, lounging on the built-in sofa after pouring myself a glass of their best red wine. They live well, these women.

What does it mean that I won't let them control me any longer? I'm not giving up my work as an artist, but I won't let it take me over again as it has in the past. I want to be open to other possibilities, just as I am when I'm creating something. No more pushing away relationships or opportunities that don't fit into my narrow artistic scope.

And Stephen? What role does he have in my future?

Only he can answer that. He's not likely to give up his life as a pastor, husband, and father. I've been a passing fancy, but it would destroy all he has built if he were to leave that world behind him. He'd never forgive me for that.

We could go on indefinitely in this limbo state, but I don't like keeping our relationship hidden. We can't be seen publicly together. What kind of existence is that?

19th Day

I slept in one of the empty staterooms and had the best rest I've had since coming aboard. No one banged on the door and asked me to make breakfast. Instead, I found a tray covered with white linen waiting for me when I got up. On it was my breakfast: warm oatmeal, some canned peaches, and coffee.

It's such a relief to be out of that muslin rag I've worn since coming aboard. I found a royal blue caftan similar to what Circe and Tarista are wearing, and it's so much more comfortable.

I haven't seen or talked to my shipmates since yesterday, but I assume they'll deliver me to my home soon. I have mixed feelings about that. My relationship with art and Stephen has shifted, and I don't know what my future will hold.

But the fog seems to be lifting, and through the porthole I can see the sun for the first time in days.

BETTY WICK

Springtime Dream

 SONYA PLENEFISCH

THREE POEMS

THE FALLING COSMONAUTS

It is early October when Komarov and Gagarin fall through my roof
like silent twin trainwrecks,
brushing off the iron stardust and asking pale-faced directions
home,
to a country that has ceased to exist.

All roads lead to Rome, but none
across the sea to Baikonur.
No land for the space-frozen Soviets.

Sometimes, I am reminded that we cannot end the war
until we bury all the dead.
Komarov and Gagarin
set up camp in my backgarden.
At night, I hear their voices burn like perpetual supernovae.

FOREST OF THE WORDLESS

~~I run out of words on Wednesday, so on Thursday~~
~~someone rings up the Secret Police,~~
~~who bundle me in a van and take me where they take everyone~~
~~who runs out of words.~~
~~A wide, wide forest, deep~~

                              underground.
Thousands of the wordless.
Artificial wind moving through, and the lonesome song it makes[1].
We all just stand there, staring at each other.
The woman in front of me has incredibly long lashes,
thick black-on-pink like newborn calf.
I find myself wishing she would skitter or huff or even just nudge me
with a black, wet-velvet nose.

---

1   Choral and electronic/ and coming from the place/ the universe just/ ends.

MARS

Imagine you're sent on a mission to Mars/ you and some other person/ some nervous boy with a twitchy hand and too-straight hair/ and when you get to Mars your spaceship breaks/ so you're there/ two on a planet/ and you're lining up rocks to spell out a message/ the way they do when they're stranded in the movies/ and you're playing with rocks and not looking when he trips and maybe there's a ledge/ a cliff/ an unfortunately placed boulder/ regardless/ he snaps his neck on the plains of Mars.

And then there was one.

Imagine you're lining up rocks for passing spaceships/ and there's this empty shell of a once-was at the bottom of a cliff or wherever/ and you realise you're the only person alive/ on this great red planet.

Contributors' Notes

alexcintron is a writer/surrealist from Ohio.

Devon Balwit teaches in Portland, OR. She has six chapbooks and two collections out or forthcoming, among them: *The Bow Must Bear the Brunt* (Red Flag Poetry); *We are Procession, Seismograph* (Nixes Mate Books), and *Motes at Play in the Halls of Light* (Kelsay Books). Her individual poems can be found in *Phantom Drift*, as well as in *The Cincinnati Review*, *The Carolina Quarterly*, *Fifth Wednesday*, the *Aeolian Harp Folio*, *Red Earth Review*, *The Fourth River*, *The Free State Review*, *The Inflectionist Review*, and more.

Adrian Blevins is the author of *Appalachians Run Amok*, winner of the Wilder Prize, forthcoming soon from Two Sylvias Press; *Live from the Homesick Jamboree*; *The Brass Girl Brouhaha*; and the chapbooks *Bloodline* and *The Man Who Went Out for Cigarettes*. She is the recipient of many awards and honors including a Kate Tufts Discovery Award, a Rona Jaffe Writer's Foundation Award, a pushcart prize, a Cohen Award from Ploughshares, and a Zone 3 Poetry Award. A co-edited collection of essays—Walk Till the Dogs Get Mean: Meditations on the Forbidden from Contemporary Appalachia—was published in 2015. New poems have recently been published in *The Baffler*, *Gettysburg Review*, *Greensboro Review*, *Southern Cultures*, and other magazines. She teaches at Colby College in Waterville, Maine.

Adam Byko is an MFA candidate and Provost Fellow with the University of Central Florida. His fiction has previously appeared in the Fall 2018 issue of *The Pinch*.

A collection of **Michael Brosnan**'s poems, *The Sovereignty of the Accidental*, was published by Harbor Mountain Press in 2017. My poetry has appeared in various literary journals, including *Confrontation*, *Borderlands*, *Prairie Schooner*, *Barrow Street*, *New Letters*, *The Moth*, and *Rattle*. He authored *Against the Current*, a book on inner-city education, and serves as the senior editor for Teaching While White (www.teachingwhilewhite.org).

Chris Bullard lives in Collingswood, NJ. He received his B.A. in English from the University of Pennsylvania and his M.F.A. from Wilkes University. Finishing Line Press published his poetry chapbook, *Leviathan*, in 2016 and Kattywompus Press published *High Pulp*, a collection of his flash fiction, in 2017. His work has appeared in publications such as *32 Poems*, *Green Mountain Review*, *Rattle*, *Pleiades*, *River Styx* and *Nimrod*.

Brent Canle is a poet from Long Island who holds an MFA in Poetry from the University of North Carolina Wilmington and is currently working on an MA in English from the same university. His work has appeared in magazines such as *2River View*, *Angry Old Man*, *The Newer York*, and others. A lyrical essay is forthcoming in *Bull Magazine*.

Matthew Chamberlin lives in Virginia, where he also writes. His stories and poems can be found in *Jersey Devil Press*, *A-minor*, *Typehouse Literary Magazine*, and other places.

Robert Cole has writing featured in *Connotation Press*, *Five 2 One*, *Cicatrix*, *Sein und Werden* and other journals or magazines. He currently lives in Valley View, Texas.

Brittney Corrigan is the author of the poetry collection *Navigation* (The Habit of Rainy Nights Press, 2012) and the chapbook *40 Weeks* (Finishing Line Press, 2012). Her poems have appeared widely in journals and anthologies, and she is the poetry editor for the online journal *Hyperlexia*: poetry and prose about the autism spectrum (hyperlexiajournal.com). Brittney lives in Portland, Oregon, where she is both an alumna and employee of Reed College. For more information, visit brittneycorrigan.com.

Susan DeFreitas has never been able to choose between fantasy and reality, so she lives and writes in both. A first-generation American of Caribbean descent, she is the author of the novel *Hot Season*, which won the 2017 Gold IPPY Award for Best Fiction of the Mountain West; her fiction, nonfiction, and poetry has been featured in (or is forthcoming from) *The Writer's Chronicle*, *The Huffington Post*, *The Utne Reader*, *Story Magazine*, *Daily Science Fiction*, and *High Desert Journal*, along with numerous other journals and anthologies. In 2017, The Oregonian named her "One of 25 Oregon Authors Every Oregonian Must Read."

Harrison Demchick is the author of the 2012 literary horror novel *The Listeners*. His album *Otherguy* dropped quietly, even silently, in 2018, and his first feature film, *Ape Canyon*, is currently in post-production. Harrison is also a developmental editor who has worked on more than seventy published books. He's accepting new clients in fiction and memoir at the Writer's Ally (thewritersally.com). "Magicland" is the title story of a short story collection in progress. Another *Magicland* story, "The Bead," will appear in the Winter edition of literary magazine *The Hunger*. Visit www.harrisondemchick com!

Linda Dove holds a Ph.D. in Renaissance literature and teaches college writing. She is also an award-winning poet, and her books include, *In Defense of Objects* (2009), *O Dear Deer* (2011), *This Too* (2017), and the scholarly collection of essays, *Women, Writing, and the Reproduction of Culture in Tudor and Stuart Britain* (2000). Poems have been nominated for a Pushcart Prize and the Robert H. Winner Award from the Poetry Society of America. She lives with her family and two Jack Russell terriers in the foothills east of Los Angeles, where she serves as the faculty editor of *MORIA Literary Magazine* at Woodbury University.

Rob Wilson Engle is an editor and personal trainer currently residing in Brooklyn. His work has appeared or is forthcoming in *DIAGRAM*, *Reality Beach*, *F(r)iction Online*, *Profane*, *Phantom Drift* and elsewhere.

Dan Frost lives in Antigua, Guatemala and Denver, Colorado. He writes poems in both places.

With poems having appeared in *Ploughshares*, *Prairie Schooner*, *Radius*, *The Oregonian*, *Commonweal*, *Southern Poetry Review*, *Southern Humanities Review*, *Spoon River Poetry Journal*, *Passages North*, *Paradise Review*, and many other places, **John Garmon** serves student writers at the College of Southern Nevada, Las Vegas.

James Grabill's recent work appears in *Caliban, Harvard Review, Terrain, Mobius, Shenandoah, Seattle Review, Stand*, and many others. Books—*Poem Rising Out of the Earth* (1994), *An Indigo Scent after the Rain* (2003), Lynx House Press. Environmental prose poems, *Sea-Level Nerve*: Books One (2014), Two (2015), Wordcraft of Oregon. For many years, he taught all kinds of writing as well as "systems thinking" and global issues relative to sustainability.

Jenny Grassl was raised in Collegeville, Pennsylvania and now lives in Cambridge, Massachusetts. She received her M.F.A. in poetry from Bennington Writing Seminars, and her B.F.A. at the Rhode Island School of Design. Her poems have appeared in various journals, including *Radar Poetry, Clarion, LIT, Pierogi*, and *Critiphoria*. She was a runner-up for the Grolier Prize in 1998 and a semi-finalist for the National Poetry Series book contest in 2003. Recently, she attended a Colrain conference.

Jonathan Greenhause was the winner of *Aesthetica Magazine*'s 2018 Creative Writing Award in Poetry, the 2017 Ledbury Poetry Competition, and the 2017 *Prism Review* Poetry Contest. His poems have recently appeared or are forthcoming in *The Carolina Quarterly, december, The Fiddlehead, The Rialto*, and *Subtropics*, among others. His second chapbook, *Secret Traits of Everyday Things*, was published by Encircle Publications last September.

Carolyn Guinzio's fifth book, *Ozark Crows* (Spuyten-Duyvil, 2018), is a sequence of visual poems. I'm also the author of *Spoke & Dark*, (Red Hen, 2012) selected by Alice Quinn for the To The Lighthouse/A Room Of Her Own Prize, and three other collections. My work has appeared in *Agni, Bomb, Boston Review, Harvard Review, The New Yorker*, and many other journals. My website is carolynguinzio.tumblr.com.

Kristen Havens' work has appeared in *Bracken, PANK, Concis*, and *The Fourth River*, among others. She lives and writes in Los Angeles.

Satoshi Iwai was born and lives in Kanagawa, Japan. He writes poems in English and in Japanese. His English work has appeared in *Phantom Drift, FLAPPERHOUSE, Small Po[r]tions, Your Impossible Voice, Poetry Is Dead*, and elsewhere.

Daniel Jaffe compiled and edited *With Signs and Wonders: An International Anthology of Jewish Fabulist Fiction* (2001), and is author of the novel, *Yeled Tov* (2018); the novel-in-stories, *The Genealogy of Understanding* (2014), the short story collection, *Jewish Gentle and other stories of Gay-Jewish Living* (2011), and the novel, *The Limits of Pleasure* (2010).

Joan Eyles Johnson lives in a little cabin in the San Bernardino National Forest and writes short stories, poems, and plays. Her work has been published in several literary journals: *Mediterranean Review, Fiction Southeast, Confluence*, et al, and four of her plays have been performed off-Broadway. In 2016 she won the Ernest Hemingway Prize for short fiction.

Joy Kennedy-O'Neill's stories have been published in *Nature, Strange Horizons, Flash Fiction Online*, and the *Cimarron Review*, among others. She lives on the Texas Gulf coast and teaches English for a small college. She is the 2018 Gris-Gris Flash Fiction Award winner, and a 2018 finalist for the Lascaux Prize in Flash Fiction. More of her work can be found at JoyKennedyOneill.com.

Gregory Kimbrell is the author of *The Primitive Observatory* (Southern Illinois University Press, 2016), winner of the 2014 Crab Orchard Series in Poetry First Book Award. His poems have appeared or are forthcoming in *The Disappointed Housewife, Manticore—Hybrid Writing from Hybrid Identities, Mirror Dance, Alcyone, Whatever Our Souls, Parentheses, Blackbird*, and other publications. He is the events and programs coordinator for Virginia Commonwealth University Libraries. More of his writing, including his magnetic sci-fi/horror haiku, can be found at gregorykimbrell.com.

Rick Krizman writes music, stories, and poems and holds an MFA in Writing from Pacific University. His fiction has appeared in *The Wising Up Press, Sediment, Flash Fiction Magazine, Star 82 Review, Medusa's Laugh Press, Driftwood, Switchback*, and elsewhere, and he is a regular contributor to *The Big Smoke*. Rick is the father of two grown daughters and lives with his wife and other animals in Santa Monica, CA.

Jennifer Lynn Krohn was born and raised in Albuquerque, New Mexico. She earned her MFA from the University of New Mexico, and she currently teaches English at Central New Mexico Community College. She was the winner of The Golden Key's 2017 Flash Fiction Contest and has published work in *Coffin Bell: A Journal of Dark Literature, Storm Cellar*, and *Tinderbox Poetry Journal* among others.

A retired educator living in a small town in Eastern Oregon, **Jack e Lorts** has appeared extensively, if infrequently, over the past 50+ years in such magazines as *Arizona Quarterly, Kansas Quarterly, English Journal, Agnostic Lobster, Fishtrap, Oregon English Journal, Oregon East* and *High Desert Journal*, among others. Many of his recent Ephram Pratt poems have appeared online in *Haggard and Halloo, Elohi Gadugi, Literary Juice* and elsewhere. Author of three chapbooks, *The Daughter Poems & Others...* and *The Meeting-Place of Words*, published by Pudding House, and *Dear Gilbert Sorrentino & Other Poems* from Finishing Line Press. Active in local and state Democratic politics, he served as Mayor of Fossil, Oregon for many years, currently lives in The Dalles, OR.

Jennifer MacBain-Stephens lives in Midwest and is the author of four poetry collections: *Your Best Asset is a White Lace Dress* (Yellow Chair Press, 2016), *The Messenger is Already Dead* (Stalking Horse Press, March 2017), *We're Going to Need a Higher Fence,* tied for first place in the 2017 Lit Fest Book Competition, and *The Vitamix and the Murder of Crows* (forthcoming in 2018.) Her work has been nominated for Best of the Net and the Pushcart Prize. She is also the author of ten chapbooks. Recent work can be seen at or is forthcoming from *The Pinch, Prelude, Cleaver, Yalobusha Review, decomp*, and *Inter/rupture*. jennifermacbainstephens.wordpress.com/

A Canadian by birth, **Lily Iona MacKenzie** has published reviews, interviews, short fiction, poetry, travel pieces, essays, and memoir in over 150 American and Canadian venues. *Fling!*, one of her novels, was published in July 2015 by Pen-L Publishing. *Curva Peligrosa*, another novel, was published in September 2017. *Freefall: A Divine Comedy* will be released in 2018. Her poetry collection *All This* was published in 2011. She taught rhetoric at the University of San Francisco for over 30 years and currently teaches creative writing at USF's Fromm Institute for Lifelong Learning. When she isn't writing, she paints and travels widely with her husband. lilyionamackenzie.wordpress.com.

Joshua McKinney's fourth collection of poetry, *Small Sillion*, is forthcoming from Free Verse Editions in 2018. He is the co-winner of the University of Georgia Press Poetry Series Open Competition, the Dorothy Brunsman Poetry Prize, the Dickinson Poetry Prize, and a Gertrude Stein Award for Innovative American Poetry. His work has appeared in such journals as *American Letters & Commentary*, *Boulevard*, *Colorado Review*, *Denver Quarterly*, *Kenyon Review*, *New American Writing*, and many others. He teaches poetry writing and literature at California State University, Sacramento. A longtime student of Japanese swordsmanship, he is a member of Senkakukan Dojo of Sacramento.

Sarah Paley is a writer who lives and works in NYC. Her work has been published in *The New Yorker*, *Barrow Street*, *Agni* (online), *Best American Poetry* blog and other magazines and journals.

Pattie Palmer-Baker is artist and poet. Although she often combines these two forms of expression in collages of paste paper and calligraphy, the inspiration for and the meaning of the artwork lies within the poem. Not all her poems appear in her artwork, but her artworks always include her poetry. Nominated for the Pushcart Poetry Prize, and published in *Eholi Gadugi Journal*, three *Poeming Pigeons Anthologies*, *Petals in the Pan Anthology*, *She Holds the Face of the World in Her Hands* (best of Voicecatcher), *Conclave*, *Spring 2016*, *The Ghazal Page*, *Voicecatcher*, *Calyx*, *Voices – The Art and Science of Psychotherapy*, *Halcyon Days* and more. First prize winner in 2016 *Timberline Review* and second prize winner in *The Highland Park Review*. Third prize winner in the Oregon Poetry Association contest.

Michigan poet, **Lynn Pattison**'s work has appeared in *Phantom Drift*, *Rhino*, *Smartish Pace*, *Tinderbox*, and *Slipstream*, among others, and been anthologized in several venues (most recently in the *NASTY WOMEN POETS* anthology and in *plein air*, poems and drawings of the natural world, edited by Arlan Miller and Susan Gundlach, Poetic Licence Press. She is the author of three collections: *tesla's daughter* (March St. Press); *Walking Back the Cat* (Bright Hill Press) and *Light That Sounds Like Breaking* (Mayapple Press).

Caroline Plasket's poems have been published or are forthcoming in *Compose*, *WomenArts Quarterly Journal*, *The Tishman Review*, *The Bookends Review*, and *The Hollins Critic*, among others. She was a fall 2016 mentee in the AWP Writer to Writer Program.

Sonya Plenefisch was raised in Sylvania, Ohio, but now lives in Brooklyn, NYC, after graduating with a BA in Design for Performance in the UK. Her work has previously appeared in *Words Dance*, *Cactus Heart Press*, *Epigraph Magazine*, *Right Hand Pointing*, *Driftwood Press and Clover*, *A Literary Rag* and *Corvus Review*.

Donna Prinzmetal is a poet, psychotherapist and teacher. She often uses writing to facilitate restoration and healing in her psychotherapy practice. Her poems have appeared in many magazines including *Prairie Schooner*, *The Comstock Review*, *The Cincinnati Review* and *The Journal*. Her first book, *Snow White, When No One Was Looking*, was published with CW Books in May of 2014.

F. Daniel Rzicznek is the author of three poetry collections, *Settlers* (forthcoming from Free Verse Editions/Parlor Press), *Divination Machine* (Free Verse Editions/Parlor Press) and *Neck of the World* (Utah State University Press), as well as four chapbooks, most recently *Live Feeds* (Epiphany Editions). He is coeditor of *The Rose Metal Press Field Guide to Prose Poetry: Contemporary Poets in Discussion and Practice* (Rose Metal Press), and his recent poetry has appeared in *West Branch*, *Colorado Review*, *Willow Springs*, *The Adroit Journal*, *The Collagist*, and elsewhere. He teaches at Bowling Green State University and lives in Bowling Green, Ohio.

Ryan Scariano's chapbook, *Smithereens*, was published by Imperfect Press. Some of my recent poetry has appeared or is forthcoming in *Basalt*; The Willow Springs Books anthology: *Heart of the Rat*; *Verde Que Te Quiero Verde: Poems After Frederico Garcia Lorca*; and *Bright Bones: Contemporary Montana Writing*. I have an MFA from Eastern Washington University and work at Eastern Oregon University.

Robin Scofield, author of *Flow* (Street of Trees Projects) and *Sunflower Cantos* (Mouthfeel Press), has poems appearing in *The Cimarron Review*, *descant*, and *Lummox*. Poetry editor for *BorderSenses*, she writes with the Tumblewords Project in El Paso, where she lives with her husband and her Belgian Shepherd dog.

C.J. Spataro is the MFA program director at Rosemont College and the editorial director of Philadelphia Stories and PS Books. She is a Pennsylvania Council on the Arts grant winner, and her short fiction has appeared in *Iron Horse Literary Review*, *Switchgrass Review*, *Pithead Chapel*, *Cahoodaloodaling*, *Permafrost*, *The Baltimore Review*, *Painted Bride Quarterly*, and others. Poetry has appeared in *Ovunque Siamo*. Her work has also been anthologized in *Another Breath*, *Forgotten Philadelphia*, *Extraordinary Gifts*, and *50 Over 50*.

Juned Subhan is a writer from England, a graduate from the University of Glasgow, Scotland, with an MA Honours in English Literature and Sociology. His work [poetry & fiction] has been published in various periodicals including *North American Review*, *december*, *Poems & Plays*, *Cimarron Review*, *Louisiana Literature*, *Quiddity*, *World Literature Today*, *Bryant Literary Review* and Joyce Carol Oates's *Ontario Review* amongst others. He is currently editing a novel.

Tim Suermondt is the author of four full-length collections of poems: *Trying To Help The Elephant Man Dance* (The Backwaters Press, 2007), *Just Beautiful* (New York Quarterly Books, 2010), *Election Night And The Five Satires* (Glass Lyre Press, 2016) and *The World Doesn't Know You* published by Pinyon Publishing in late 2017. His fifth book *Josephine Baker Swimming Pool* will be released in 2018 by MadHat Press. He has poems published in *Poetry*, *The Georgia Review*, *Ploughshares*, *Prairie Schooner*, *Blackbird*, *Bellevue Literary Review*, *North Dakota Quarterly*, *december magazine*, *Plume Poetry Journal*, *Poetry East* and *Stand Magazine* (England), among others. He is a book reviewer for Cervena Barva Press and a poetry reviewer for *Bellevue Literary Review*. He lives in Cambridge (MA) with his wife, the poet Pui Ying Wong.

Sara Moore Wagner is the Cincinnati based author of the chapbook *Hooked Through* (Five Oaks Press, 2017). Her poetry has appeared in many journals and anthologies including *Gulf Stream, Gigantic Sequins, Alyss, Reservoir, The Wide Shore, The Pittsburgh Poetry Review*, and *Arsenic Lobster*, among others, and she has been nominated for a Pushcart prize. www.saramoorewagner.com.

Betty Wick's art has been thoroughly influenced over the years by early Mexican Women Masters. These dedicated artists worked boldly with large colors, back dropping detailed lines. Wick emulated their formats, and made it her own creative launching pad. The use of black and white was a natural evolution for her. She tended to lean towards the fantasy end of the spectrum, and was not a stranger to pareidolia impressions. More at www.bettywick.com

Charles Wilkinson's publications include *The Pain Tree and Other Stories* (London Magazine Editions, 2000). His stories have appeared in *Best Short Stories 1990* (Heinemann), *Best English Short Stories 2* (W.W. Norton, USA), *Best British Short Stories 2015* (Salt)and in genre magazines/ anthologies such as *Black Static, The Dark Lane Anthology, Supernatural Tales, Theaker's Quarterly Fiction, Phantom Drift* (USA), *Bourbon Penn* (USA), *Shadows & Tall Trees* (Canada), *Nightscript* (USA) and *Best Weird Fiction 2015* (Undertow Books, Canada). His collection of strange tales and weird fiction, *A Twist in the Eye*, is now out from Egaeus Press. A full- length collection of his poetry is forthcoming from Eyewear. He lives in Wales.

Accepting Submissions for Issue No. 9
January 1 - April 30, 2019

Please read guidelines carefully before submitting, then submit your fabulist story, poem, or critical essay for Issue #9 through our website at:
www.phantomdrift.org

Fiction:
$5 per page (minimum $10)

Poetry:
$5 per page (minimum $10)

Nonfiction:
$5 per page (minimum $10)

WE AT
PHANTOM DRIFT

GIVE A MONSTROUS

SHOUTOUT

TO CONTRIBUTORS,
DONORS AND
SUBSCRIBERS,
FOR BELIEVING IN US.
WE COULDN'T MANIFEST
WITHOUT YOU.

THANKS!!!

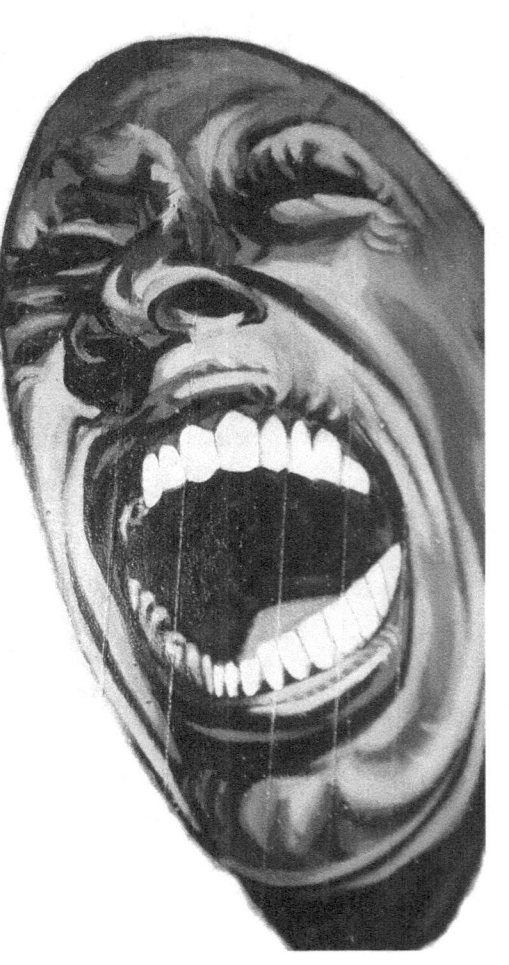

www.ingramcontent.com/pod-product-compliance
Lightning Source LLC
Chambersburg PA
CBHW080819250626
47159CB00011B/3447